THERE'S NO PLACE

TALES OF HOME BY STORYTELLERS WHO HAVE EXPERIENCED HOMELESSNESS

Edited by HE Casson

Cover art, design, and typesetting by Nathan Fréchette. Edited by Molly Desson and Joel Balkovec.

Legal deposit, Library and Archives Canada, November 2023.

Paperback ISBN: 978-1-990086-52-6 - Ebook ISBN: 978-1-990086-63-2

Renaissance - pressesrenaissancepress.ca

Renaissance acknowledges that it is hosted on the traditional, unceded land of the Anishinabek, the Kanien'kehá:ka, and the Omàmìwininìwag. We acknowledge the privileges and comforts that colonialism has granted us and vow to use this privilege to disrupt colonialism by lifting up the voices of marginalized humans who continue to suffer the effects of ongoing colonialism.

Printed in Gatineau by
Imprimerie Gauvin - Depuis 1892 – gauvin.ca

THERE'S NO PLACE

TALES OF HOME BY STORYTELLERS WHO HAVE EXPERIENCED HOMELESSNESS

Edited by HE Casson

with stories by
Alice G. Waldert – Cait Gordon – K.A. Wiggins
Jamieson Wolf – Karin Hedetniemi – P. E.
Marco Katz Montiel – Kasimma – Brandon Case
Cassandra Mangano – David Hankins – Em Dupre
Elysia Willis – David Simmons – Koji A. Dae
Eddie Generous – Anne K. Spollen – Carlin Dixon

Renaissance acknowledges the support of the Canada Council for the Arts.

Conseil des Arts
du Canada

Canada Council
for the Arts

For Chandrahas—wherever *you* landed,

for Pablo—*where* the best stories *live,* and

for Graeme—*where* I found home.

CONTENTS

PREFACE

H. E. Casson

As humans, we survive best when we are able to create tapestries of interdependence with each other, within our communities, and with our broader environment. The warp and weft of our tapestries may tie to family members, workplaces, or religious, cultural, and social communities. There can be smaller threads, like the coffee shop where they know our order, or the valley where we can name the trees. When we're safely wrapped in this protective fabric, we may not even realize how interdependent we are, how interwoven.

The longer we stay in one place, the thicker our threads can grow and the more of them we have. We are crisis-resistant when our tapestry is strong and diverse. A snipped thread or a skipped stitch is less likely to unravel us. We can even become other people's threads, supporting those around us.

To be homeless is to have those threads cut, sometimes one after the other, sometimes all at once. We may struggle to re-weave and replace, and the tapestry will never look the same.

Yes, home is a tenuous notion. It's the subject of a thousand glib sayings and a thousand more remarkable selections of art and story. Author L. Frank Baum had his young Dorothy declare, "There is no place like home." Van Gogh painted what he called "people's nests", noting the similarities between the homes of wrens and those of local families. Inaugural poet Maya Angelou, who crashed in a junkyard as a teenager, declared that, "the ache for home lives in all of us..."

I believe that people who have lost home pen some of the boldest, broadest, and most inventive portraits of what that word can mean. The absence of society's easiest, default concept — a safe box inhabited by the resources and beings needed to get along in life — necessitates a creative reimagining of home's definition.

For me, home has been the floor between my cousins' beds, and the bag of candy I hid underneath. It's been a pull-out couch in my teacher's basement. It's been a pilfered collection of poetry, an army surplus backpack, a public park climber, a subway train. More-so, it's been people: the librarian who introduced me to the poet; the found family who rode the subway with me; the community member who spotted me the cash to buy the backpack; the sanctuary of my favourite human's arms as we slept in the park. Home has been inconstant. It is ever-evolving, rediscovered or replanted as old definitions are ripped away. If you saw my tapestry, you'd find a cacophony of frayed ends, mismatched threads, and more than a few holes. Good stories can live in those holes, though.

The idea for this collection of good stories was born in 2020. That's when a stay-at-home order made it clear that home, both in our imaginations and on the ground, was not universal.

Some people were trapped in unsafe conditions, some gathered in encampments, some moved back in with family. There were folks in studio apartments, folks in multi-room houses, and folks who slept rough. Friends and family were separated or lost. Community members experienced major changes at work, at school, and in all the imperfect-but-often-life-saving havens we rely on when housing is not a sure thing. For some of us, Covid-19 entered the home of our bodies, creating changes in our senses, our physiology, our capacities, our feelings, and our thoughts.

Usually, when homelessness and housing were being discussed, reported on, and debated, the voices centred were those of politicians, homeowners, and people who work with folks experiencing homelessness. Rarely were the voices of those in the scrum brought to the forefront. In a time defined by crisis, so little was heard from those with who knew, firsthand, what surviving one requires.

Through it all, again and again, we called on our capacity for redefining home. A protest, a support group, a body that exists in a new way—these can all be home.

That is why, instead of asking for stories about homelessness when we made the call for submissions, we asked for stories of that thing we all ache for: home. In these pages you will find eighteen stories of home, all written by storytellers who have experienced insecure housing and homelessness. They have imagined home as an AI ship, a shared mutation, a bird's nest, a car, a song, a tarot card, and an alternate reality. In this collection, you will find a thesaurus of the synonyms for home.

To every storyteller who shared their work, whether they were selected for inclusion or not, I say thank you for allowing us to visit you where your writing lives. It's been an incomparable gift to look at all these tapestries, and to explore the experiences and ideas that helped weave them together.

And to the readers who now share this same opportunity, I say: welcome home.

YOUR TEACHER'S HOUSE

by Anne K. Spollen

I.

It is the middle of a cold and sunny Saturday afternoon. I park the car outside a pharmacy because pharmacies seem safe, and right now, I want safety. I am trying not to think, but all I can do is think.

Do NOT think of a yellow balloon. In your mind, a yellow balloon floats. The brain does not like tricks.

So I watch them for distraction: the connected people, the ones walking in with children and shopping bags and purpose. I sit in the car, thinking of buying cigarettes now, knowing I should not buy cigarettes.

That damned yellow balloon again.

I'm lucky I have this car. It's mid-size. It should do, at least for now.

I am watching a family walk past with bags. Look at them: intact, smiling. Nothing has gone wrong there. No knives. No heroin. No alcohol. No bruises. Nothing.

You should see the house I left last week: it's huge, so much bigger than where I grew up or have ever lived. I confused bigness with safety.

In a big house, I could never get hurt. In a big house, everything would be perfect. I would sleep with the moon over me, the stars around me, everything breathing in and out, ensconced in a cloak of hushed warmth.

But that house is no more. I can never go back there.

He waits for me in the breathing dark of that house, when I'm asleep, when I'm not looking. I had to let the house go, had to let its doors and wood and glass slip through my fingers like water.

II.

I fled that place.

Or did I? Fled is such a quick flash of a verb, even in the past tense. I saw some of this coming for the last few weeks. At night, I woke in the big house, afraid. He worked nights, but not every night, and sometimes he got off early. Those were the worst. He would use on those nights.

I thought about leaving. But where would I go? I worked part time, had a car and a degree. I tried an agency, and she told me I was wasting her time because I had no police reports.

Do you know what would happen if I had called the police? Tell the police when I cannot tell my friends? When I hide bruising from family? I would not be sitting here, writing this on a windy Saturday afternoon. Have you MET him?

We need documentation she said, tapping her pen against a clipboard. So...

How do you document fear? Oh, Housing-and-Shelter-Agency-Worker, do you want to wait until he has broken another bone, or until I am dead? No. We don't say he broke the bones. You don't know that. But aren't you trained to read between the lines? All the truth in the world quivers between those lines.

No, sorry. We say you have a job and a house. Even if the deed doesn't have your name. Even if the job is part time and you eat rice or noodles most of the time. Even if your bank account is in the double digits, you are not entitled to shelter.

III.

The day was blue and crisp when I knew I had to leave. The thought moved through me like electricity as I cleared plates and wiped counters while he watched TV.

I will leave.

Somehow.

And the electricity was all happy and bouncy, thinking I would never have to wipe these counters again, never have to stand in the kitchen making dinner, never folding his sheets, never mopping the floor.

Leave. The word. The happiness. It's possibility, and right now, possibility is everything.

Possibility is hope. It is life.

IV.

The planning begins: placing socks and underwear, deodorant and soap, little bottles of shampoo, toothpaste, sweaters, small towels, putting them inside pillow cases and hiding them around the house. Finding the backs of closets, small spaces behind chairs, even using an empty filing cabinet in my office.

I have one drawer there, shared with the other part time teachers. They keep normal things in theirs: papers, bottles of water, extra pens, files. Not me. I keep a new toothbrush, a little money, mouthwash and socks. I'm planning, planning...

I cleared the trunk of my car out, all the junk I kept in there: anti-freeze and ropes, a jug of water, clamps, ancient packets of sugar, and a blanket that smelled like oil. And then I went to find the apartment.

First and last month's rent, in addition to the current month. Can any exception be made to that?

Look, we got a lotta folks interested who have the cash...

Back home to think. Roast the chicken, wash the potatoes, fold sheets, find spaces in the car when he's not home: some cash under the floor mats, remove the spare tire and leave it next to the dumpster at work and find a whole area for toiletries, clean out the small tool kit for work supplies and a clipboard to lean on to write.

And then it happened.

He broke the door. I was asleep. He broke the door and I heard everything inside me break, including anything that held me to that place.

I got him out of the bedroom. He held a knife in his hand and said he was "kidding around" and why couldn't I take a joke?

Awake until morning, then I looked around and took some pictures, put my mother's jewelry inside some socks, grabbed two heavy sweaters and boots. And that was it. Gone.

V.

Life in a car has its advantages. No more cleaning for one, well, very little, keeping the space in a car clean is vital. The passenger side holds things I need during the day, and so far, the blankets have been enough for warmth. The back seat has laundry baskets filled with clothes; I put pillows on top of them, and it's a wide twin bed.

There are places that welcome me. Libraries have bathrooms and quiet space to do my grading, write my lesson plans, apply for jobs. They have computers and warmth. You can't eat there, but sometimes I take a few pieces of cheese and an apple and bite when no one is looking. I change libraries often; the college has one that's huge and silent.

VI.

When I stand in front of students and talk, I wonder – do they know I go home tonight to a Wal-Mart parking lot or to the hospital lot? Do they know I shower at the cheap health club and brush my teeth in their library? Do they think the person who shows them how to craft a thesis, work citations, and interpret poems rolls over at night in the backseat of a Honda, hoping blankets work for the long winter?

No, they would never think that. I stay clean and dry and put mascara and a necklace on before going into the classroom. I want to tell them people are not what you assume, that big houses are not safe, that marriage is not always a covenant, and that home is a place you carry with you.

A CHOSEN STORY

by Jamieson Wolf

Content Warning: homophobic slurs

In front of Willard's room at the Elysian Shelter, Rupert shyly handed him the deck of tarot cards. "They can be your family now," he said.

Willard looked up at his brother and tried to keep the confusion out of his voice. "Thank you?" He sighed inwardly.

Rupert reached out and ruffled Willard's hair. "Stop overthinking. I can hear the gears turning inside your head."

"Did you want to come in?"

Willard swore to himself. This was a shelter, for goodness' sake. It's not like he was welcoming Rupert into his home, but it was in a way, or as good as. He stepped away from the door, and his brother walked in.

"I can't stay long," Rupert told him.

"Oh?" He tried to keep the hurt out of his voice. He was so fragile and could not let Rupert know how even the sight of him was causing something inside to break. He could feel the small cracks, like fissures in stone, spreading along his skin.

"No one knows I'm here," Rupert said, looking awkward. "It was better this way, fewer questions."

"Of course," Willard said, the cracks within him deepening quickly. He wondered if his brother could see them, if they were shining brightly, or let out only a dull light. Willard didn't know how much light he had left.

"Why did you do it?" Rupert said in an intense whisper. "You know how Father feels about fags."

The cracks snapped audibly. "I'm not a fag," Willard said. "I'm gay."

"To-*may*-to, to-*mah*-to," Rupert said. "Call yourself what you want. You should have just stayed in the closet. It would have made things easier."

"For whom?" Willard asked, trying to keep the cracks from cutting into him. It made no difference.

"For all of us," Rupert let out a sigh. "I mean, we all *knew*—it was just easier pretending you weren't."

"Easier for *you*," Willard said. "I didn't want to pretend anymore."

"Well, now you don't have to. Good for you."

Willard lost his patience. A fissure within him opened wider and he could feel the hot lava of self-hate boiling up within him and he had to direct it somewhere. He closed his door and turned on his brother.

"Why are you even here? Did you skulk up here in the shadows, afraid someone would see you talking to a someone like me?" Willard spat. "How did you find out where I was?"

Rupert shrugged. "Aunt Cathey told me," he said. "She was very upset. Wanted me to see you, offer you some comfort."

"So that's what this is?" Willard said, brandishing the box of tarot cards at Rupert. "They're supposed to bring me *comfort?*"

Shrugging again, Rupert said "I've always found them helpful whenever I was stuck or had a question that needed to be answered. I always turned to them. These seventy-eight cards gave me help when I needed it."

Willard let out a laugh. "You expect me to believe you kept this hidden from Joyce, the religious fanatic?" he said. "She would have chucked you out if she had found them. Father and our stepmother make quite the pair. They're both afraid of their shadows but not afraid of lashing out when they feel they have just cause."

Rupert surprised Willard when he reached out and touched the large purple bruise that ran along Willard's jaw line. Willard would never tell Rupert what that touch meant to him. With the way that their father and mother had looked at him, Willard had been made to feel as if he carried an invisible disease; according to them, he *was* a carrier. They had offered to pray it out of him, and he had told them to go fuck themselves.

That was when his father had punched him.

"I'm sorry he did that," Rupert said. "I'm sorry for not sticking up for you."

Another geyser opened within Willard. "Why didn't you?" he whispered, feeling the fissures within him filling up with unshed tears.

Rupert shook his head. "You know what it's like," he said softly.

Willard nodded because he did understand. He truly did. "Why are you here? Why did you bring this to me?"

Rupert shook his head and Willard wondered if his brother was going to respond. Willard could see him trying to gather the right words, forming them in his head before he spoke them.

"I wanted to give you something to remember me by," Rupert said. "I wanted to give you something that would help you in your current ... situation."

There it was, then. This was hello and goodbye all in one fell swoop. Now Willard tried to keep the disbelief from his voice, but it came out anyway, "With tarot cards?"

"You'd be surprised," Rupert told him. "There's a lot of wisdom in those cards. They helped me a lot, and they are the most treasured thing I own. I wanted you to have them."

Willard took the tarot deck. Running his fingers over the box that had been worn around the edges. He read the words *Rider-Waite-Smith Tarot*. Opening the box, Willard shook out a stack of cards and a little white book.

"That's the guidebook," Rupert said. "I used to just draw a card and look up the answer, but then I paid attention to what I was seeing and feeling. I got better readings that way."

"You can't read cards," Willard said.

"You can read these," Rupert told him. He tapped the card that was facing them. It was a card labeled with the word Death. "These aren't just cards. These are seventy-eight windows into yourself. They helped me a lot and I hope they can help you."

Willard threw the cards onto the bed. "Thanks," he said. "That's really thoughtful," Willard said.

Rupert looked uncomfortable. "I'm sorry, Willard. I really am."

"I know you are."

But I'm not, Willard thought.

They stood looking at each other, and there were a million words unsaid between them. Willard could feel them filling up the cracks that ran beneath his skin. He could feel the word *guide* by his left knee and the word *should* lodged up his right shoulder. *Ask* was tickling his left kneecap. He could feel the word *forgive* along the length of his pointer finger.

He waited for his brother to pull him into a hug, to say something more, for Rupert to tell him that he would come and see Willard again. Rupert said none of those things, no matter how hard Willard wished for it.

Instead, Rupert said "Try and have a good life, okay?"

More words fell into the cracks like brother, *remorse* and *joy.* "You too," Willard said.

Then the door closed, and Rupert was gone.

Willard looked around the small room he was in, at the single bed and the bedside table, the small dresser that held his meagre possessions. He turned to look at the closed door and at the world he had left behind walking away from him even now. He did the only thing he could think of doing. Willard picked up the deck and threw it across the room. The cards flew into the air. He noticed a card marked with a flaming tower, and the cracks within him split apart. He knew from reading tarot cards that the Tower meant the foundations that he had built his life on were about to crumble and the Tower was going to come crumbling down. He school his head; the cards always seemed to know.

Falling onto the bed, Willard let the darkness claim him as he pondered how the fluttering of the cards reminded him of birds.

When Willard woke, the darkness was broken by a spot of light in the distance.

He looked around himself and saw only shadows. He wondered if the shelter turned off all the lights in the evenings to save electricity.

Getting up out of bed, Willard moved forward towards the light and with every step, the glow in front of him grew brighter, as if he were opening a window. Willard thought briefly of his brother and pushed it aside.

Shielding his eyes, Willard walked towards the light. He could see different colours, as if the light were being reflected through a prism. The light became even brighter the closer he came to it. Willard covered his eyes with one hand and moved closer to the light until he could not see at all. He had to cover his eyes with his hand and still he moved forward, the warmth of the light increasing with every step until it was almost burning his skin.

When Willard could bare it no longer, the light increased to a blinding flash and then was gone. He knew that it was safe to uncover his eyes because the warmth of the Sun had stopped burning him. Looking around him, Willard saw that he was in a meadow. There was grass as far as the eye could see and trees in the distance. Close to Willard, watching him with kind eyes, there was a woman who stood next to a lion.

At first, Willard thought it was his mother, but then he looked again and knew it wasn't her. The woman regarded him kindly, and Willard knew that there was wisdom there. He could see it in her gaze. She did remind Willard of his mother when he looked at her, but her face was all wrong. It was the eyes that were like his mother's—the resemblance stopped there.

He should have felt afraid, but he had stopped being afraid a long time ago. It was what had gotten him into this mess in the first place. Again, he thought of his brother and what he had said but pushed him away again.

"You know, if you keep pushing everything away, you're going to be alone," the woman said.

Her voice was not unkind, but it sounded stern, as if no one would dare to mess with her. There was a Strength that radiated from her, like his mother when she was still alive. She had been the strongest woman that Willard had known.

He approached the woman without fear. She gave him a smile and held out her hand. "Merry meet, dear boy. I was wondering which one of us you would draw."

Willard shook his head. "I don't draw. I can only do stick figures."

She let out a soft laugh that sounded like bells ringing in the air around them. The sound made him happy.

"The cards, dear boy, the cards."

She motioned at his pocket. Willard put his hand in his pocket and found the tarot deck waiting for him there.

"We all wondered which card you would draw out of the deck, you see? I'm so happy you drew my card. Being with a lion is nice and all, but he's not much of a conversationalist."

The lion let out a loud *harrumph!* and lay down on the ground. The woman sat beside him and patted the grass beside her.

"Come sit with me for a spell, dear boy."

"Why do you keep calling me that?" Willard asked, sitting down beside her.

"It's what I can see in here," she said, leaning forward to press a hand softly into his chest. "What would you rather be called?"

"My name is Willard."

"That's a fine name. Old-fashioned like mine." She held out a hand. "My name is Fortia."

Raising an eyebrow, Willard said, "That's an odd name."

"Short for *Fortitude*." She tilted her head to the right and looked into Willard. He could feel her dark brown eyes searching within him. "You've had quite the journey to get here, haven't you?"

Fortia gave him another searching look.

"You think you're done, but you're not. You've only just started on your real journey."

Willard shrugged. "You're just full of mystery, aren't you?"

The lion huffed out what sounded like snort, and Fortia threw the lion a glare that Willard's mother had often given him. It was the look that said *Shut it.*

When Fortia turned back to Willard, the fire that had been in her eyes had calmed. "I can't go giving you the whole story when you have yet to write it. But you drew me for a reason. That means that there is strength in you, running through your veins. I can tell you that much."

"Great, what am I going to do with that?"

"Well, it led you away from your family home, didn't it? You are staying in this quaint shelter, aren't you? Safe from those that would judge you."

"Kicked out, more like."

"Yes, but even so, you *went.* You didn't grovel or beg. That's not your way."

"But I cried," Willard said.

"Crying isn't a sign of weakness," Fortia said gently. "Contrary to what other people think, it's actually a sign of strength. It's a sign that you *care.*"

Willard had never thought about it that way. He had always been told that crying meant that you were weak. He had tried to keep all the tears inside of himself every time his father would yell at him or hit him. Sometimes, it felt like he was full of a river that his skin could barely contain.

"He would tell you that crying meant you were weak," Fortia said gently, as if reading his thoughts. "That's what he wanted you to think because that's what he was *told*."

Bristling, Willard said "Are you standing up for him?"

She let out another laugh that filled the air with bells and birdsong. "Heavens no! Your father was an ass pure and simple. But don't you see? He was telling the story that he had been taught, the story that had been told for generations."

She tapped his chest where his heart lay.

"What story are *you* going to tell? How will you continue your tale?"

Willard let out a laugh that rushed past his ears like a gust of wind.

"My tale is already done," he said. "There's no more story to tell."

"Oh, you think so, do you? Well, you're wrong—but that's why I'm here. Someone needs to lead you in the right direction. It might as well be me. First, let me ask: how do you love yourself?"

Willard felt the tears well in his eyes, but he would not let them fall, not yet. He hadn't been asked anything like that since his mother had been alive. He shook his head, clutching his eyes closed so that the tears would not fall.

"I don't love myself," he told her. "I'm a freak."

She patted his hand like a mother would. "Again, you're just repeating what you were told. You started a new chapter of your story, Willard. When you left home to live your life, you gave yourself a chance to begin again."

He let out another laugh, and this time, it sounded like a birdcall. "Not much of a beginning, is it? Cast out from my family and living in a shelter? Not exactly paradise, is it?"

"Even paradise must start somewhere. You did what you never thought you could do, Willard! And now look where you are! You stood up to those who wanted to keep you down. You had to stand up against what frightened you most in the world." She reached out a gentle hand and ran it along the bruises that were like bright splotches of paint on his skin. "That is the very act of self-love. You were brave enough to choose yourself."

Willard didn't know what to say to this. He was still shattered by the whole thing and usually woke from a dream of his father hitting him. Willard remembered the rage in his dad's eyes and how his father had promised to *beat the gay* out of him. It was the same dream every night. The tears did come then and though Willard wanted to wipe them away, he let them fall. They fell into his lap, resembling small diamonds.

The lion stood and came closer. It sat behind and pressed itself against Willard and commenced purring. Willard immediately felt better. He leaned against the lion and rode the gentle wave of the lion's breathing. There was something so calming about the purring of the lion and it lulled Willard into a feeling of safety that he had never experienced.

"I bet it's easier having a lion. Makes being brave easier," Willard said sleepily.

Fortia gave Willard a gentle smile. "I had to tame the lion, Willard. That didn't happen right away. It took time. Managing to overcome the darkness or difficulties in our lives isn't done with the snap of your fingers. It takes work."

"Is that what I have to do now?" he asked. Another tear slid down his cheek. "It took so much out of me to leave home."

"Of course, it did. The hard decisions in our lives take the most out of us. You have to decide which story you choose, Willard. Only *you* get to decide how it will go." She tapped the tarot cards in his pocket. "These will help you find your way."

A spark of light bloomed in Willard. "You mean they will tell me what I have to do?"

Fortia gave him a look of exasperation and leaned against the lion with him, causing the lion to let out a sigh that sounded like *oof!* Fortia turned to the lion and tapped its nose playfully. "Quiet, you. Willard, aren't you tired of being told what to do? I've told you that you get to choose your own story now. These cards are your guides along the way. Think of them like windows."

The words sent a shiver down his spine.

"My brother said the same thing."

Willard let out a sigh, and he realized the light in the sky around him was growing brighter again. As he watched, the light grew brighter, and he almost had to shield his eyes again, like he had when he had arrived here to this strange meadow. Willard looked to Fortia for an explanation and in answer, she took his hand in hers. "Our time here has come to an end, young Willard."

"So soon?"

"Dreams are like that. They are never permanent. Fear not though. If you have need of me, you can always look for me in that deck of tarot cards your brother gave to you."

The light increased, and he had to cover his eyes so he could only hear Fortia's voice.

"You will do fine, Willard. Choose your story and you will be fine. I have faith in you."

When he woke, Willard was in his room at the shelter, and it was morning.

The light streamed in through the windows. He had forgotten to close the thin curtains, not that they would have done much anyways. Sitting up in bed, he saw the tarot cards he had thrown laying scattered around the room. He got out of bed and collected them all one at a time. When he was done, he counted them. Rupert had said that there were seventy-eight of them, and he counted seventy-seven. He looked around the room and spotted a card lying in front of the door, as if it were heading outside.

Picking it up, he was not surprised to see that it was the Strength card. "Hello, Fortia," Willard said.

He rubbed his thumb over the lion. Looking down at the card, he thought it was a sign that he was going to be okay. He put the card with its brethren and closed the box top.

Willard went to the window and looked out into the world that, until now, had seemed so large and frightening. It still was, there was no denying that, but now Willard wanted to know how he would make his mark in the world and what kind of story he would grow to tell. He knew that there was a lot of work ahead of him but all he could do was take it one day at a time and find the way. He would go wherever his story took him.

Willard thought he could hear the sound of bells and the soft purr of a lion coming from somewhere inside of him and Willard felt calm. He could *do* this.

"Thanks, Fortia," he said.

MOURNING DOVES, COME BACK TO ME
by Marco Katz Montiel

The site of violent death now remains tranquil, a silent memorial to itself. This morning, I step out on the patio to contemplate it once again, thinking about all that has recently passed in this once inconsequential place.

We plan to leave in a few days. Still feeling privileged to have lived for a time in this gorgeous setting, we are saddened to have our last days shadowed by the tragedy that befell creatures, who had captured our hearts. For we know that, wherever the paths away from this place take us, those two parents will continue to mourn so deeply that it makes them abandon, at least for a time, their eponymous song.

Will they come back next year? Will I or any human here ever again see one of those dark round eyes peering back? My wishes matter little. At the end of this week, new tenants will move in, and if they even notice the return of these neighbors, whom they will never have known, they will have no reason to seek me out to provide an update.

Yesterday afternoon, I stood in the same place, quietly cooing to the home that they have left—cooing to myself, really—and wondering if these neighbors who have lost so much could ever bring themselves to return to this spot and try again. The thought seems incredible, but they have surprised me once before and, even though this seems that much more farfetched, I like to suppose it could happen one more time.

Earlier that afternoon, I had swept up the remains of the second corpse, long skinny entrails, looking more like worms than guts, with a few decorative feathers spread about. I thought that this could have provided a final bit of sustenance for the ravenous beast that had torn this tiny body apart. Why did it leave that edible portion? Perhaps something had come along to scare it off prematurely.

She hated the sight of it. Please pick it up and throw it in the garbage, she told me.

I didn't want to tell her my thoughts, which seemed silly, even in that moment. I wanted to take the remains out back and bury them. If I did this, I could stand looking ridiculous in her eyes and those of anyone she might tell, knowing that deep down she understands this part of me. But we have so much to do this week, packing up our own residency here, giving things away when we can, throwing out the rest, and then having it all nice and clean for the next tenants. Still, I could not just throw what was left into a dirty brown plastic garbage container and let it sit inside there until the trucks came by to mechanically load it in the back and haul it off to a dump. Instead, I placed the feathers and thin trail of intestines on a plate, took them out back, and placed them under a hedge. There, they could nourish the ground or maybe some other scavengers, hopefully not the killer, likely to frequent that part of the yard.

ॐ भूर्भुवः स्वः ।

तत् सवितुर्वरेण्यं ।

भर्गो देवस्य धीमहि ।

धियो यो नः प्रचोदयात् ॥

Although I chanted this "Gayatri Mantra" many times to the doves as they took turns with their offspring, I did not do so yesterday morning when one of them returned briefly to sit on a branch above their now abandoned home. This time the mother or father had its own song to sing, a short coo sounded repeatedly with brief spaces in between. Perched above the home built with care, it mourned. As usual, there was nothing useful for me to add to this situation, so I stood quietly and tried to emulate the posture of Kurdish fighters I see leaning slightly forward in news photographs, the ones who know how to passively share in active mourning.

The day before yesterday, she and I, devasted by the first slaughter, went out for an evening walk, talking about the sudden event that had changed the lives of our neighbors on the patio. We noticed a profusion of angry sparrows flying around above us. Did they know that we had failed to protect the vulnerable avian young in our midst? Although not of the same species, they might have cared. But no, it had nothing to do with us; none of this really has anything to do with us, at least not in the sense that we can make a difference. A hawk had perched in front of one of the sparrow nests and ate calmly, as if at a smorgasbord.

You see, I told her, it wasn't a crow but a hawk, and here it has gone right on to kill again. With some trepidation, I walked up to the ravenous beast and, seeing that it feared me, yelled, clapped my hands loudly, and chased it away. As it headed to a nearby tree branch, followed by dozens of chirping sparrows, I decided to wait until the hawk gave up and went further away—although, I knew, it could still come back after I left.

25

What are you doing? she asked. It has already done away with its victim. You should let it finish eating. After all, it's another wild animal that deserves to live. You're right, I replied. I know that I have no right to this vengeance that, after all, accomplishes nothing useful, but even so, it makes me angry to see this after it has just killed one of the babies that we care about so much. No, it didn't, she insisted. That was a crow. I saw a big black bird fly into the patio, and this bird is light brown.

I don't want to believe this. She used to keep the cat inside when crows were around because some news article had convinced her that those birds were that powerful. She even said once that they could take away a human baby, but this did not seem possible.

I don't want to stop loving crows.

In the afternoon, before our walk, she and I threw a going-away party for ourselves. Friends came by to share food and drink, listen to music, laugh, and talk about the past here and times to come in other parts of the world. After going for a swim in the community pool, we returned to our indoor dining area. Normally, we would have sat out on the patio on a day so beautiful. Now I wish that we had done so that afternoon.

With one guest left, she looked out the window and noticed a sudden movement. Run, she told me, go out there now. The cat must have gone after the doves, I thought insensibly as I headed out the door. I thought this even though I know that Frodo is one of those felines incapable of jumping or climbing even an inch above his own head. But what could it be? Just after she told me to run, I had seen a shadow fly across the window, but had not connected it to the swirl of confusing events that I tried to process in that moment. Without allowing any of these thoughts to make me hesitate, I ran to the patio.

We were too late. Only one young dove was left. The other had disappeared, carried off by a crow, she said. I couldn't believe that anyone from my beloved murder had perpetrated this horror. The crows I see and hear every day make lots of noise, happily bothering neighbors but delighting me with their wild ways. I have never seen them hurt anyone.

लोकः समस्ताः सुखिनो भवन्तु)

Our yoga teacher tells us that this prayer, "Lokah samastah sukhino bhavantu," calls on us to make all of our thoughts and actions increase the freedom and happiness of all creatures. As much as I would like to pray for this sincerely, the idea has always made me uneasy. How can we hope for this in a creation filled with contrary interests?

Two months ago, our feathered neighbours came back! Their arrival filled me with joy, and I ran into the house to tell her about this. That's no surprise, she said. They built a nice home here, and it served them well. They had two babies, the way they were supposed to, and raised them in a safe and peaceful place until they could go off on their own. Now they're ready to do it again, this time without having to start from scratch.

Not necessarily, I admitted. I was afraid that my intense interest had frightened them off for good, and that they would prefer to find another place to make a home. You never interfered with them, she assured me, and it looks as though your watchful chants didn't bother them. If you're concerned about it, she added, you can back off a bit this time.

Happy to see these beautiful visitors again and loving the unexpected return that made it possible for me to once again enjoy their presence, I felt thankful for the dark causes of my own peregrinations. This time, we had less than a month instead of the year granted us earlier, so the incredible coincidence of our arrivals meant all the more to me.

Just under a year earlier, the first pair of young doves left for good. I had watched them impatiently wait for their parents to bring them food, then venture out on their own to sit on nearby branches. They began to figure out this world so new to their weeks-old eyes. They must have realized, one day, that their parents would not come back with more food, advice, or encouragement, so they made their final departure. In that last moment of their tenancy, I came as close as I had ever come, pleading with the last young one to stay. You should live here, I sang seductively, this could be your home. Clearly frightened, the young bird flew away more quickly than I had imagined possible, making me wonder if any of them would ever forgive my stupidity and give the place another chance.

ॐ ॐ ॐ शान्तिः शान्तिः शान्तिः ॐ

Without any other common language, I hoped that this "Om Shanti Om" sung in ancient Sanskrit would make sense to our new neighbors. I chanted these calls for peace and understanding so often that I thought they had become used to my voice and presence in their proximity. After many disillusions, how is it that I continue to believe in these delusions?

Several months before I watched the young doves depart, I observed the parents build their home. Near the end of winter, which is not a severe season here, they came with twigs and bits of leaves and other stuff found on nearby yards, expertly weaving as pretty a home as I had ever seen. After a couple of days, they took turns sitting there, and it became clear to us that they were hatching something.

As anyone might gather from the name given to their species, they did not look particularly happy. (How many young couples of any kind really look happy while setting up their first home?) Their distinctive cooing pattern tipped me off, and I used that hint to go online and search the name: *paloma de luto*, as people say here, or mourning dove. Their very appearance expressed all of the sadness heard in their habitual song, but they worked with zest and ambition. It made me think that the creation of this nest—on which they would (according to a trustworthy website) take turns sitting on the two eggs destined to be hatched there—gave them a sense of satisfaction and maybe even pleasure.

Having learned of the itinerant ways of mourning doves, I felt some commonality with them, having been forced earlier in life to move from place to place. We hoped that the new neighbors would come back once more before we departed for good. We loved this Spanish-style home with a patio so enchanting that we had accepted the owner's offer without looking inside. We ate all of our meals outside, feeling transported to our old haunts in Valencia or one of the prettier places in Madrid. Knowing from the beginning that our residency would not last long, we decided to enjoy it thoroughly.

As city people who usually enjoy crowds of humans, we found the swarms of other animals delightful. Our lack of knowledge, we reasoned, could be made up for with a concomitant effort to avoid interference with this suburban landscape and its non-human inhabitants. We pulled out the dead ferns that even we knew never had a chance in this desert environment and, with advice from a gardener from Durango, put in bougainvillea, hibiscus, jasmine, and honeysuckle, all plants that flourished with a minimum of human care. Hummingbirds came by to suck nutrition from the flowers and drink clear water from the small recycling fountain that also provided a soundtrack for the patio. When I sang along with my guitar, they sometimes lit on branches or hovered in midair with an expression of interest that surprised and delighted (and likely deceived) me. Neither she nor I set out seed or sugar water, so these unexpected avian visits made us especially happy.

Sparrows came by from time to time, along with other birds we could not identify. The crows made their presence known for much of the day, but never flew into our patio. Once in a while, a bunny rabbit would stick its nose through the iron gate, and we saw roadrunners pass by, but mostly those ground-hugging creatures made up for their inability to fly by staying away. Coyotes prowled around, as well, and we felt glad that any creatures finding their way into the walls of our patio did not have to worry about them. Without a specific intention, we found ourselves inhabiting what looked like some nineteenth-century painting of a tiny prelapsarian corner.

Before moving here, like other people who inhabit cities, we would only take short trips to less crowded places. It had not occurred to us to leave our cozy apartment filled with books to spend the better part of a year in the suburban outskirts of a small southern town until one day, a disease came along that sickened fellow humans and left many dead. Not having obtained doctorates or any other type of qualifications in medical care, we could do little aside from staying in touch with friends, donating modest sums of money, and continuing to maintain connections, now forced online, with our students. The crisis kept people in their homes, which created an opportunity for those of us able to function from a distance.

It will be idyllic, she told me, and I had to agree. A place so beautiful and comparatively isolated might prove boring to some, but we felt sure that our active intellectual life would prevent that sensation. Also, we looked forward to meeting new neighbors. In any case, we would not have to directly face tragic realities back home. Our spirits hopeful, she and I excitedly packed a few items indispensable for daily life, gathered a large number of books, and took flight.

BENEATH A VEIL OF SNOW

by Brandon Case

An icy gust of wind cut through the spring morning like a scythe, tearing young leaves from their stalks and curling around the exposed neck of a young girl.

Aina sucked in a startled breath. "The air tastes like icicles!" she said, opening her mouth for another bite.

"Come inside, Aina," her mother called from their cottage. "My bones ache. This spring is fragile."

The breeze tugged at Aina's blue dress and tangled in her long, dark hair.

"No!" I want to play with the wind."

"You aren't dressed for this weather—and I don't want you catching cold."

Aina stuck her hands in the pockets of her dress. "If I get cold, I'll hug Theodor."

"Don't talk nonsense." Her mother leaned through their cottage's small, square window and scowled. "An imaginary bear can't keep you warm."

"He's a *magic* bear. You wouldn't understand."

Her mother's expression darkened—the lines of her face as craggy and sharp as the frosted mountains. "Magic isn't real. She pointed to a stand of birch at the forest's edge. "Cut yourself a switch and get in here. *Now.*"

Aina's stomach twisted, and she gasped rapid, shallow breaths that made her dizzy. But Theo's lessons kicked in, and she bared her teeth.

"Never! I'll have my bear eat you!" she shouted, sprinting into the trees.

"Get back here, Aina!" her mother shouted. "You have nowhere to go!"

Aina dodged through the underbrush, weaving into the forest's ensconcing darkness. Soon, a hulking, black shape loomed in the shadows. Theo was enormous today, standing on his hind legs and pawing at a beehive thirty feet above the ground.

"My favorite human!" he said in a deep, rumbling voice. "Mind the bees."

Theo dropped down, making the pines shake and drop a cascade of golden needles. He ambled over and looked closely at Aina, snuffling her face. "What's wrong?"

"Mother doesn't believe you're a magic bear." Tears slid down Aina's cheeks. "Now she's going to whip me."

"That woman," Theo growled. "She doesn't deserve such a good daughter."

Aina hugged him, nuzzling into his soft, black fur. Theo put an enormous paw on her back and held her until she stopped crying.

"I hate it," Aina said. "Being afraid. Being punished. I'd give anything to be free of this place."

"Where should we go, Little One?" he asked.

"Let's find a hill with a meadow. I want you to taste the wind. It's like icicles. You'll love it."

"Sounds crisp enough to crunch," he rumbled. "I do enjoy when breathing is a feast."

Aina motioned for him to come closer. Theo's body shrank now that she was calm, becoming Aina's height, and she put an arm over his shoulder. They hiked up the foothills in search of a nice, open spot.

The temperature dropped but the hike kept Aina warm. Her breath puffed out in big, white plumes. She laughed and blew mist at Theo. He returned the favor, huffing out an enormous cloud.

Aina wrinkled her nose and giggled. "Your breath stinks, Theo!"

"I thought it'd be sweet," he grumbled, "especially after eating all that honey."

They marched for hours, heading steadily upward. The first two hills they passed offered no view of the sky or taste of the wind. However, the third crest was entirely bare, like a bald head with a crown of conifers.

Aina stepped into the meadow. A jagged gust of wind at cut her face, making her gasp. It tasted like frozen metal instead of the crisp flavor of icicles. She looked up at the craggy mountains, and her stomach twisted.

"N-No," she whispered.

Black clouds dominated the sky, towering above the peaks. Billowing, white haze swept down the slope: a blizzard as dense as an avalanche, poised to crush them.

The storm's violence paralyzed Aina. Her father's red face flashed across her mind, followed by her mother brandishing a birch switch.

"We should go back, Little One," Theo said.

The bear grew and grew with her fear, gaining fifty feet of height and blocking Aina's view of the storm. Her paralysis ebbed, and Theo gently guided her into the woods.

The trees dampened the wind, and Theo shrunk to fit between the pines. He walked ahead of Aina, retracing their tracks up from the valley.

"I don't have to go back to that house, do I?" Aina asked after a while.

It was warmer under the canopy. Perhaps they could simply make a fort and weather the storm.

"I do love the forest," Theo said. "Maybe we could build a home here."

They followed their old footsteps onto one of the forested hills and stopped to survey the area. Aina collected several fallen limbs and leaned them against a tree. She covered the gaps with smaller branches, adding layers of wood until it was difficult to see through the barrier. Satisfied, she crawled into her fort. Theo shrunk to the size of a baby bear and curled up on her lap. She patted his fuzzy head, feeling proud and sufficiently protected.

However, sitting still let the cold to catch up with Aina. It wound around her, seeping through her shelter and into her skin. The forest was strangely silent, absent even the small sounds of scurrying animals. She heard every needle that fell into the pine straw.

Aina shivered. "I'm cold, Theo."

"I like your fort, Aina." He peered out at the first snowflakes drifting through the trees. "But we might want to move somewhere warmer for this storm."

Aina scowled. "Do you have somewhere in mind?"

"I saw a cave in the first hill we crossed. Caves are great for winter. I hibernate in one when we aren't playing."

Aina crawled out of her lean-to and looked up at the sky. Clouds blotted the sun, tinting the world with harsh steel gray. Fat snowflakes fell in earnest, and the treetops whipped back and forth. She shivered, fear prickling her arms. Theo grew to the size of a grizzly.

Wind grabbed Aina's dress as she hurried through the trees, hands curled deep in her pockets. Theo lumbered ahead, examining the ground. A fresh layer of snow obscured Aina's trail from earlier.

Her friend grumbled while deciphering their path. "I'm shocked that your mother doesn't believe I'm a magic bear."

"I know! Not only can you change sizes—" Aina pointed at the unblemished layer of snow beneath Theo "—You don't even leave footprints!"

"I'd like to see a normal bear do that!" he said.

Aina shivered. "Theo, I saw my father's face earlier."

The bear let out a low, throbbing growl. "Don't worry, Little One. He died years ago."

"Yes, but I saw Mother right after, and it wasn't much better."

"He lingers in that broken woman. Remember what I taught you: if threatened, get big and fierce. Most predators will back off."

Aina bared her teeth and brandished her fingers like claws.

"Perfect!" Theo said.

Aina stuffed her hands in her pockets. "My fingers feel weird, Theo. Tingly—like little shocks. My toes, too."

He nodded sagely. "That happens to me after collecting honey. The bees sting, you know."

Ribbons of white wind hissed through the trees, laden with bands of snow. Underbrush snapped against Aina—a thousand little whips, flogging her legs. She sniffled and wiped her nose on her shoulder.

Theo stopped. "You're too cold."

"Ye-yeah." Aina marched in place, her teeth chattering.

"Here," Theo said, reaching behind a nearby tree and producing a coat of black fur. "It's my daughter's. I'm sure she'd want you to wear it."

Aina slipped into the jacket. It fit perfectly—and while it didn't stop her from shivering, she felt a bit better.

"Thank you, Theo."

"Let's hurry to the cave, Little Bear."

They scrambled downhill, stumbling over rocks hidden beneath a layer of fresh snow. Aina's legs moved sluggishly, heavy and wooden and never quite landing where she intended.

"Theo, look!" She pointed ahead.

The ground rose sharply on the far side of a ravine. A dark recess lay halfway up the hill, framed by two enormous stones.

Aina missed a step and crashed down the slope. Tree limbs bludgeoned her sides, she slammed into a boulder, and finally hit the bottom. She lay in the gulch, sprawled on her back.

"Aina! Aina!" Theo stood above her front paws held to the sides of his face in horror.

"I-I'm." Aina struggled to her knees. "I'm..."

"Your legs are bleeding and you're covered in snow!"

"I-I'm okay." She stood shakily. "I'm okay. I barely feel it."

"Let's get up to the cave," Theo said.

Aina nodded and laboriously climbed out of the ravine. She struggled to keep her legs moving, eventually crawling on hands and knees to make it up the hill. Finally, she slipped into the cave entrance. It was dark inside. A creepy, living blackness that coils around the soul and whispers with the sweetness of rotting meat. But the stone walls blocked the howling wind, and it *was* warmer.

Aina curled up in the entryway, with her back to the tunnel descending further into the rocks.

"Aina, you probably shouldn't lie down..."

"I'm too tired, Theo." She brushed clumps of snow off her dress, tucked the fabric around her legs, and snuggled deeper into her fur coat.

Theo huffed, but lay against her back, becoming the perfect size to hug her.

Her hands and feet stopped tingling. They barely felt cold anymore.

Aina's eyelids drooped, extraordinarily heavy. They closed and she slowly forced them back open. She knew she shouldn't sleep ... but a nice, slow blink couldn't hurt.

"Aina!" Theo stood above her, yelling her name.

"Go away, Theo. I'm sleeping."

"Get up, Aina," Theo insisted.

She curled tighter. "Sometimes you're more badger than bear."

"The storm is worse. Snow is coming into the cave, and you're too cold again."

"I don't feel cold," she said.

"Just go a little deeper into the cave. It might help."

Aina's limbs moved like wet clay: heavy, bendy, and blunt. She crawled into the darkness. A deep, rumbling growl echoed through the chamber. Aina froze, sure it was the sound of Death, opening a crack in the earth to swallow her. Her heart pounded and a rush of adrenaline lifted the fog from her mind. Ahead, a pair of eyes glowed in the blackness. Another deep, menacing growl reverberated through the cave. The points of light crept closer.

Aina screamed and scrambled back; Theo grew explosively.

"I don't fit!" The bear collapsed, too big to stand in the cavern. "Aina, let me shrink."

She backed away, staring at the approaching eyes. They passed beyond the shadows, revealing an enormous mountain lion. It slunk toward her, body low, muscles rippling, ready to leap forward and sink its teeth into her throat.

Theo's body ballooned. His head swelled until it filled the cave, pinning her against the wall. Instead of crushing Aina, she merged into Theo with a little *pop*. She was inside the bear's head but could see through him, and the air shimmered as though viewed through a rainbow.

The lion was gone, replaced by her father. He stalked forward, red-faced and glowering, fists balled at his sides.

Aina cringed away, tiny, useless, stuck.

"You can do this, Aina." Theo's voice spoke directly into her mind. "You've become a strong bear. Show him."

Slowly, Aina rose. She raised her arms overhead and brandished her fingers like claws.

"Get away from me!" she screamed, showing her teeth. "Don't ever touch me again!"

Her father stopped advancing and took a step back.

Theo shrunk. Once their bodies separated the prismatic veil fell away. The man before Aina disappeared, replaced by the lion. It hesitated, considering her.

Aina's bear stood beside her, teeth flashing in the dim light. Theo *roared*, shaking the cave. Aina leaped forward to back him up, shrieking and waving her arms.

The lion retreated into the shadows, its eyes flashing.

"Let's go," Theo said.

They exited the cave into a full-on blizzard. Snow and ice blasted Aina sideways. She tried to grab a tree to steady herself but couldn't grip it.

"I can't make my hands go back to normal," she shouted over the wind, holding out her claw-like fingers.

"Your fingers are black, like mine!" Theo held up his paw to show how his inky digits matched the color of her skin. "Maybe you really are turning into a bear."

"Where now?" Aina asked, shoving her twisted fingers into the dress.

"It's time to go home. We can deal with your mother after the storm."

Aina slogged through snow that came up to her knees, fighting to summit the hill as violent gusts of wind buffeted them against trees. She crested the rise amidst a rising dread. The air was solid white: an opaque veil that closed less than ten feet ahead. She spun in a circle but couldn't tell which way led down to their cottage in the valley.

Cold and exhaustion dragged Aina to her knees, and she suffered a strange urge to burrow into the snow and pile it over her like a fluffy, white blanket.

"You have to keep moving, Aina." Theo grew to the size of her entire house. "Just a little further. I promise, things will get better."

"I trust you, Theo."

Aina pushed herself up and crept forward, weaving through the pale pines as though drunk. Her father appeared before her once more, stepping through the shifting bands of snow. The red of his face glowed against the white haze. She flinched. The sight of him made her stomach twist with fear ... but if she stopped moving, she'd never be able to start again.

"Get out of my way." She growled and brandished her blackened fingers. "You're dead and I'm a strong bear."

Her father laughed. "You're a stupid little girl, dying in the woods alone. Did you forget everything I taught you about frostbite?" He pointed at her blackened claws "How about hypothermia? Hallucinations?"

Aina's eyes wouldn't focus. She concentrated on placing one foot in front of the other, leaning into the wind.

"What about paradoxical undress? Have you had the urge to burrow, yet?" he asked. "Your heart is weak. I'm sure it's failing. Just let go."

"You aren't here," she said to his image. "I watched that tree crush you, and I did not weep."

"Maybe not," her father said. "But it won't be long before you crawl under a bush to join me."

Aina bared her teeth and shoved past him with all her strength. She lurched forward, and her foot sank through the snow without stopping. There was no ground, just white powder piled against a cliff. She fell, plummeting downhill, picking up speed, ricocheting off trees, knocking the air from her lungs. Her bones crunched as she bounced between boulders, tumbling and tumbling, down into a clearing, her limbs flopping at awkward angles, until she rolled to a stop.

Everything was wrong.

Her right arm bent backward at the elbow, and her feet refused to move. Her blue dress had come up and tangled around her throat. Theo bent down, nudging her with his nose.

"I'm sorry, Theo," Aina said. "I probably ruined your daughter's coat."

"You *are* my daughter, Little Bear."

"I-I think I'm dying, Theo." Tears trickled down Aina's cheeks and fell into the snow, melting little holes. "I can't feel anything."

"I'm so sorry," he said, gently setting his forehead against hers.

Aina choked back a sob. "Is what my father said true? Am I all alone out here ... or are you really a magic bear?"

"Don't worry, Aina, I'll always be with you. And what is magic, if not a bit of comfort and love?" Theo placed a paw next to Aina. "I think it's time I show you more of what I can do."

He grew, expanding and expanding until he was the size of a mountain, and his body filled the entire valley. Just the tip of his claw was bigger than a house.

"Come, Aina." Theo's voice rumbled like distant thunder. "It's time."

Aina crawled forward, dragging her useless legs. She hugged the enormous claw. With a small pop, she passed into Theo and found herself in another world.

Warmth rushed into her. The storm broke and every trace of snow disappeared. Sunlight shone on green spring grass, waving lazily in a gentle breeze. Aina felt strong and soft, although somewhat lower to the ground than usual. The fur coat had expanded, completely covering her skin. She reared back on two legs and pawed at her round, furry ears and snuffly snout.

Colors shimmered in the air, more beautiful than anything she'd imagined. The smell of wildflowers drifted around her, each scent so strong and vivid it was like a thread leading back to the flower. A breeze brushed her fur like a trusted hand.

"It's beautiful, Theo!" Aina ambled into the valley, immediately recognizing the landscape. Someone had replaced the awful birch trees with a field of blueberries, but this was definitely her home.

She approached the little cottage, and her mother appeared in the window, looking younger and happier—like the days before her father lost his job and started drinking. Relief flashed across the woman's warm face.

"Aina, you're home!" Her mother ran to the door. "I was so worried."

Aina stood on her hind legs and put her paws on her hips. "If I'm coming home, you have to promise there'll be no more hitting."

"Of course!" Her mother gestured to the missing birch trees. "You're safe here."

"And I'm a magic bear, now. So you have to believe in us."

The older woman nodded enthusiastically. "Come in, come in. You've had a long day."

Aina nosed past her. A fire crackled in the hearth, and the house smelled like bread and roasting meat.

"Can I get you anything?" her mother asked.

"I could use a nap," Aina said, heading to her room.

Her mother opened the door for her with a smile.

Aina climbed into bed and burrowed beneath soft white covers that rustled and snapped like the branches of a bush. A deep peace stole over her, entirely warm and free of fear.

"Thank you, Theo," she whispered.

Perfectly content, she closed her eyes. As her mind dimmed, Aina caught the crisp flavor of icicles on the air. She hoped Theo could taste them, too.

JUST LIKE CAMPING

by Cassandra Mangano

I wake with the electric shock that something's wrong. I look around my tent taking inventory before I realize the high-pitched sound I'm hearing is Petey yelling my name. I stretch out in my sleeping bag, so cold it feels wet, and run my hands over the plasticky floor, the concrete slab under it making it that much colder. Everything's still dry, and I think to myself it's a minor miracle we haven't had rain all week.

Petey is still shouting, alone in the next tent where he and my mother sleep.

"Okay, buddy. Give me a minute," I call over to him. His yelling continues.

I linger on the last moments of the day I'll have to myself, screaming child or not; the time before I leave my tent is still *my* time. The smell of sweaty clothes combines with an old apple core by my head and makes me want to gag. Petey is louder now that I have acknowledged him, showing off, wanting attention. This is the routine every morning after Mom leaves for work.

I unzip the flap door and stick my head out. The odor of the pit wafts through the air, smelling of urine and feces and slightly of fish, the way outhouses do in summer heat. The sun is fighting to break through a gray-blue mist of cloud cover overhead, and the garage bays are still dark. I scan for glowing eyes. Even here, so close to downtown, wild things need shelter.

Barefoot, sleeping bag in my arms, I tread lightly on sharp rocks over to Mom's tent. Petey stops yelling like he always does the second I touch the zipper. He runs to the door, wraps his arms around me, and clings, so I have to pry him off my neck just to get through. I duck in and clear a place on the crowded floor, spreading my unzipped bag over me so it's wide enough for Petey to come under too. The smell is worse in here. Clothes are strewn about, food designated to a corner but surrounded by dirty and clean dishes. Mom let go of the idea of organization months ago, and now I think she's just happy the mess doesn't draw pests. Petey watches me, holding his sleeping bag at the center of his chest like a bath towel, and I realize, with an ache that hurts worse than my empty stomach, how much I want a shower.

I slap the space next to me, and Petey jumps to the floor. He snuggles under my outstretched arm like a kitten, and I hug him close, trying to warm him up. Last week, we were waking up sweating, and now Petey's shivering, covered in both his bag and mine.

"Kara?" Petey asks, looking up at me with his large brown eyes.

"Hmm?"

"When are we going home?"

I tell him what I always do. "We're going to have a new home pretty soon, but it's not ready yet."

"Oh yeah," he says, remembering again. "And I'm going to have my own room. And a lots of toys. And—" he pauses between words the way little kids do when their brains are moving too fast for their mouths. "And I'm going to have a race car!"

"Oh yeah?'

"Yup! And it's going to be even better than the other house, right?"

"Yup!" I echo.

"Even better than Daddy's house?"

Spit sprays over my lip a little as I let out a hard laugh, "Yeah, Petey. I'm pretty sure it's going to be better than Daddy's house."

He wraps his little arms around me as far as they'll go. When he starts squirming, I ask, "Bathroom?"

Petey kicks off his bag like he's on a mission and bolts out of the tent so fast he's almost to the pit when I call him back.

"Petey! T.P.?" I yell.

He makes a dramatic U-turn, snatching the roll out of my hand, turns and runs even faster.

I sort through clothes looking for something for him to wear, already knowing nothing is clean; more than that, nothing will fit. Petey has grown so much in the last year. He still looked like a toddler before we started staying at the garage, and now, in a couple of weeks, he'll be starting kindergarten. I don't mention school to Mom. She's already pulling triple shifts at the diner, taking time off to look at apartments with broken staircases and black mold growing inconspicuously in the corners of the bathroom ceilings. School means school supplies, backpacks, and Petey with nothing to wear. She didn't need a reminder.

Petey's been wearing shorts for months, but the way the wind is blowing this morning tells me those days are officially behind us. I find an extra-large sweatshirt and a pair of jeans that were baggy on him a few months ago. There's a big mud stain on the butt, but other than that, they look clean.

Petey comes barreling into the tent the same way he left, tripping over the pile of clothes and falling into the soft mound. He rolls over, moving his arms and legs in wide x shapes. "Making clothes angels," he says.

I hand him the outfit and turn to our food stash for breakfast. The only things left are two rolls, grown hard and stale from last night's dinner, a bag of chip dust, an apple, and a jar of peanut butter. Even though she works three shifts a day, Mom is only allowed one meal. She brings it home to share, always something with veggies, salad, or stir-fry, leftover broccoli from the steam table, overcooked and gray, the texture of applesauce.

I help Petey wash up before I take the rolls, smear them with big spoonfuls of peanut butter and hand them both to him. His long shirt looks like a nightgown on his tiny body, but it covers the stain on his pants. He crunches into the hard bread without complaint. It's funny how easily people could get used to things, even picky kids like Petey. For myself, I choose the apple, bruised and rotten on one half. I cut away the worst parts and put peanut butter on it to cover the mealy texture I know it will have before I even bite into it.

"Can we go to the park today?" Petey asks, wiping his peanut butter hands on his pants.

"Maybe. We have some things to do first," I say, and make my way back over to my tent.

I rummage through my things. Besides my clothes, I have a few books, my backpack, and my camera. It's an old Nikon my grandfather gave me when I was twelve, the year before he passed away. It's still his camera to me, something I love and take care of for him. I remove it from its case and examine the lens. It looks, I think, like new. I hang the strap around my neck and head back outside. The sun is shining, uninterrupted now, and I smile up at it, thankful again for the lack of rain.

The sun warms us as we walk toward town. Petey holds my hand in a vice grip. I'm thankful for this clingy phase; it makes it easier to keep track of him. Still, I wonder if it's something we should worry about. Is he being sweet, or is he holding on to me so tightly because he's afraid of what might happen if he lets go?

We walk along the sidewalk until Main Street comes into view, then we turn toward the little gas station on the corner. Really, the best station in town is the fancy one off Second Ave. It has big, handicapped bathrooms with sinks large enough for me to fit my whole arm in. But the owner caught on fast, told us they weren't a personal bathhouse, that if we wanted to use the bathroom, we had to buy something. I think it was the wet hair that did it. Since then, I've learned my lesson and save my shampooing for when mom can get enough time to take us to a friend's house.

The bathroom at the little gas station is small enough that my knees touch the sink when I use the toilet, but Annette, the owner, never minds us coming in. I think we could probably wash our hair there if we wanted, but I don't want to push our luck. Today, Annette offers a grandmotherly smile and offers Petey a piece of candy from a miscellaneous jar on the counter. She extends it to me too, but I politely refuse. The smell of Petey's apple candy is enough to break my heart, just a little, as I leave the store empty-handed.

Mom knows a guy; that's how we're staying at the garage. That's how a lot of things get done in our town. Someone knows someone who can help with something. It's never much, but usually, it's enough. When our last slumlord shut the water off and moved out of state, Mom told us to pack *just the essentials* and talked to a guy she knew.

"It's just like camping!" she had said at first, trying to make her exhausted face look chipper.

It hadn't been like camping, though. It was not fun or whimsical. We could not just pack up and go home when we got sick of the bugs or the rain or going to the bathroom outside; there was no place to go. Now, after nearly four months, I'm right there with Petey, wondering when we will be allowed to live indoors again.

Mom knows a lot of people in town, and so a lot of people know us. We're *neighbor kids* to them. Me and Petey, and Jacob Pierce and his brother Jim, and Betty Alley, and a handful of other street scrappy kids. People wave to us but keep their distance. I don't mind if people think I'm a neighbor kid, but I wish they wouldn't think it about Petey. He's still so young; he doesn't need anyone thinking he's anything just yet. We don't hang out with those kids, we never did, but that doesn't matter.

Gage, the pawn shop owner, doesn't like doing business with minors, but he deals with us because he thinks we're neighbor kids, and neighbor kids keep his head above water. They're the ones pawning their grandparent's old jewelry for a cheeseburger. Or a gram of seedy weed from Danny Bridges, who doesn't care how old someone is as long as they keep their mouths shut.

I take the camera off my neck and place it delicately on the counter. Gage eyeballs it silently. He takes it out of the case, flipping it around as if to say, *Is this it?* I keep my head up, ready to protest.

"People aren't really buying these anymore," he says, putting it back in the case. "Everyone has a camera in their pocket."

"What can you give me?" I ask, and my stomach flips because I know whatever number he says is going to be too low for my grandfather's camera. I also know no one else is going to want it.

Gage looks over at Petey, who's running his hand along a row of CDs, trying to keep himself occupied. The way he's looking at him, focused, unblinking lest he misses the moment Petey sticks something in his pocket, up under his baggy shirt, makes me furious. I don't really blame him, though, not if I'm being honest. It doesn't matter that he knows us, knows we've always been good kids. Good kids change fast around here. Still, this is Petey, who wakes up every morning crying for his mommy and holds me so tightly with his little fingers that my hands go numb. I'm ready to take my camera and leave, call it a wash, when Gage speaks up.

"I'll give you fifteen bucks."

My eyes well with tears, but I don't let them fall. I'm still doing business here. I scan the room, looking for anything I can trade.

"What about that little DVD player," I say, thinking maybe I can flip it.

"Forty," Gage says flatly and moves away from the counter a little, letting me know this transaction is finished, that he's not going to haggle.

"Gage!" I groan, "No one's buying DVD players anymore, either."

"Forty."

I push my fingers into my eyes to keep them from tearing up and look over at Petey. He's found an old clacker toy in bright primary colors and is whacking the balls together with crazy jerking arm movements.

"Put it back," I say, but Gage waves his hand, signaling he can have it.

I breathe in slowly, "Alright. I'll take fifteen," I tell Gage, "but on loan."

I touch the neck strap of the case with affection, promising myself I'll come back, knowing I probably won't. I hold my hand out for the cash.

The fifteen dollars is unbearably light in my pocket as I lead Petey down the street toward the thrift store. A red truck creeps behind us in the parking lot, like they're checking to see who we are, and I freeze up. It's not *him*, though, just an older lady looking for a parking spot. Petey doesn't say anything about the truck, doesn't point at it or stop or scream or cry. I'm glad for all those things. I don't want to think about Robert, not yet.

Maybe clothes shopping is too strong a word for what we do at the thrift store, but when we leave, Petey is up one whole outfit, his first day of school outfit, and that's worth something, right? Maybe. But it's not worth much.

We're back at the garage with the sun setting behind us before I realize we've skipped lunch. My heart sinks, and I remind myself to take better care of Petey from now on. We look in the food pile together for a bite and find very little. Like an answer to our question, headlights illuminate the walls of the tent, blinding us briefly. Mom's home early from work. She gets out of the car carrying a bag, and without knowing what it is, my stomach starts to flip, the Pavlovian response to any promise of food these days.

She pulls two boxes from the bag. In one box is grilled chicken and rice, and I thank the gods of American dining for their generous serving sizes. The mashed broccoli is there as usual. The other box is full of dinner rolls, already growing stale. I can't keep my eyes off the chicken. I watch it, hoping my hungry glare isn't edging over into greed. It hurts how much I want it. My body needs protein so badly I can feel it in my skin, in my veins, like an addiction. I turn away from the meat and look at Mom. She leans in close so Petey won't hear her, not that he's listening. He's preoccupied, tearing at a piece of chicken with his hands.

"I think I got a good lead on a place today," she's smiling. I smile back and nod but don't allow myself to share her optimism. *The road to Hell is paved with good leads*, I think.

I bite into a small piece of chicken, and my head swims. It's like the feeling of a splinter coming out of your skin or breathing after holding your breath for a long time. Instant relief. I want to cry; it's so good. Mom gestures toward the food. Petey is digging into the rice with a black plastic fork, holding his head above the box and shoveling it into his mouth, letting bits fall away, scooping them back up like it's a race. I look down and do the math on the remaining food. Enough for one person and a quickly growing boy, not more. I shake my head.

"I ate something earlier," I say, not technically lying. "I actually have some place I have to be."

"What place?" Mom asks, scrutinizing me.

"There's this thing—" I begin, "at school. It's kind of like an open house for freshmen?"

Mom gets quiet and looks away.

walk the five blocks to a dilapidated apartment complex where a red pickup, rusting at the wheel wells, sits in the driveway.

"Hey kid!" Robert beams as he opens the door wide for me to step in. He's happy, I'm guessing about four beers happy.

"Hi Dad," I say, and cringe at my weak little voice. I think of Petey and step into the dark apartment, unable to look Robert in the eye. He reaches for a one-armed hug, and I let him.

"So, what's good?" he asks, closing the door behind us.

I don't answer. I don't know what's good. I can't think of anything.

"So—" he pauses, "high school this year, huh? You must be excited." He reaches into the fridge for another beer, straightens up, and extends one to me with a boyish, sideways grin. When I give him a look, he withdraws, quickly saying, "No. You're right."

"That's kind of why I'm here. School, I mean," I'm trying to get to the point, but it's harder than I thought. Satisfied with what he thinks I'm saying, he takes a seat in a recliner that seems to be stuck in recline.

"Your mom send you crawling back here to beg for money, is that it? You want to look good for those high school guys?"

"What? No," God, the look on his face makes me want to puke. "It's Petey."

Robert's features stiffen. "How is Peter?" he asks in a serious tone.

I can feel my eyes wanting to roll, but I keep my thoughts to myself. Insulting him isn't going to help me. I take a deep breath and stick to the truth. "He's getting big," I pause, weighing my next words carefully. "He misses you."

"I bet he does. I bet you all miss me when you need something." He cracks the beer and takes a long pull, letting it trickle down his beard onto his neck and faded blue tee. "You know," he says, voice low now, almost a whisper, "I never wanted this."

The pitiful way he's looking at me is enough to soften my resolve altogether. I look around the apartment, at the empties and the pizza boxes and the sink of crusty dishes, the cat food dish, belonging to no cat I've ever seen, that looks like the most sterile thing in the place, and I think that maybe when a guy is this low, when he has this little, the best thing to do is let him be. I turn to leave without saying goodbye.

"Wait, wait," Robert says, groaning, swinging his lower body over the extended legrest and moving toward the kitchen. He pulls a coffee can down from the top shelf of a cabinet, opens it, and pulls out a fifty-dollar bill, waving it at me. I approach cautiously, more than half expecting him to pull it away as some sort of cruel joke for me trying to leave him, but he lets me take it. He holds my hand for a second, forcing me to look into his sad, wide eyes. "Don't say I never did anything for you," he says and turns away.

Outside, the air feels clear. I have to stop myself from running, screaming with joy. I thrust the fifty in my pocket and hold it there just in case it decides to run away before I get to spend it. In my hand, fifty bucks feels like fifty thousand, like the cure to all our problems.

When I get back to the garage, Mom and Petey are already in bed, a flashlight glowing softly from the inside. I unzip my tent and crawl into the pitch-black.

"How was it?" Mom yells over to me.

"Better than I expected," I say, happy I don't have to lie.

I crawl into my bag with my clothes on, hoping to stay warm through the night. I won't tell Mom about Robert until I buy Petey his stuff. I reach into my pocket again, making sure the bill is still there. I run my fingers over it, giggling lightly so Mom doesn't hear. In the next tent, she's reading a story to Petey low enough, so I can't make out which one it is. Petey lightly cracks his clapper toy like a metronome along with her words. I sigh and smile, and let myself cry just a little. I hold the bill like a promise and drift into sleep feeling so light that nothing, not even the sound of rain coming in hard and fast in the distance, can ruin my night.

THIEF

by Elysie Willis

It had been an average day when Agnes first saw the lights. That morning, she'd woken early to make scones for the Ladies' Bridge Club breakfast. She'd headed out in her old sedan and driven to the market on the corner, where the man behind the counter greeted her by name. She bought some sugar free lemonade, then headed to the First Episcopal Church on Main to meet up with the girls as she did every Saturday morning. She spent the day making small talk and discussing their next game, then stopped by her nephew's house to give him the leftover scones to share with his wife. After, she'd come home and watered the plants before making a simple dinner for one.

Not a single thing out of the ordinary.

She'd been doing the dishes when she spotted it at the end of the driveway, three red flashes in rapid succession. Lost in thought as she was, caught up in the soul music playing on the old record player behind her, Agnes wasn't sure if the flashing had occurred before that moment. She watched and waited for it to repeat, transfixed on the inky night.

A minute or two passed, and Agnes nearly brushed it off as her imagination, until she saw it again. A red flash. One, two, three — then darkness. Agnes leaned forward and squinted into the shadows. She couldn't see much out there, but the unknowing made her chest tighten. Was there someone at the end of her drive? She couldn't be sure, but she went to check the locks.

On her way to the front entry, a pounding knock nearly sent Agnes out of her skin. She ceased her approach and waited, frozen, pulse rushing in her ears. She thought the deadbolt looked secure, but now she couldn't be certain.

Knock. Knock. KNOCK.

Agnes hurried to the door and twisted the lock as far as it could go before peering out the peephole. Her porchlight was on, but she couldn't see anyone standing there. Not that that meant no one was. There were bushes to the side, out of her range of sight. It would be easy for someone to hide, waiting for her to open the door.

Agnes swallowed, checked the locks again, then turned off the porch light. When no third knock came, she headed to the back entrance and was horrified to find that that door was indeed unlocked. She never left it unlocked. Where had her head been?

Agnes slid the lock into place right as this door, too, received a demanding knock. Agnes stumbled back, her chest aching with the frantic beat of her heart.

"I'm calling the police!" she shouted, but didn't immediately move. Instead, she waited once again, listening for any signs that whoever was out there was trying to break in.

From the backyard, more red lights flickered in the distance, flashing one after the other in quick bursts of three. Agnes drew her blinds and finally went to the phone, but when she lifted it, there was no dial tone. Instead, it sounded as if someone were breathing on the line — slow, unsteady breaths like they'd been running but were trying to hide it.

Shaking violently now, Agnes considered taking her vehicle to the police station, seeking help in person. But whoever was doing this was out there. What if they caught up to her before she even reached her car?

The red lights, though muted by the blinds, continued to flash. Agnes turned off the living room lamp as well. The house was dark now, but for her bedroom. Agnes checked the phone again — nothing but a dead line. Behind her, the soul singer continued to croon, but there was a warped quality to her voice now, like the record had overheated.

Agnes turned off the music and hurried to her room. Minutes passed without incident, but she was unable to relax without knowing what had happened to the person outside. She found herself holding her breath, clinging to the silence with hope.

But it was ripped away from her with the sound of a crash.

It sounded like it had come from the living room, shattering glass. A window breaking. Agnes ran to her bedside table and grabbed a pair of sewing scissors. It was the only defence she had, and her bedroom door had no lock. If someone were in the house, they'd be able to get in.

The phone, like before, appeared to be out of service, and Agnes had no exit route. Her house was only one storey, but for an elderly woman, a fall from those high windows, should she try to crawl out of one, would surely be disastrous. Agnes clutched the scissors firmly and waited for the sound of movement in the house.

It felt like hours had passed when Agnes slowly pushed the bedroom door open. She maneuvered down the hall, searching for signs that she wasn't alone. Her fingers tingled where she'd gripped the scissors so tightly, her free hand along the wall, steadied her quaking steps. She'd sneak through the house, then hurry to the car. If someone were inside with her, it was her only choice. Better than sitting around, vulnerable to the stranger's whims.

Nothing appeared broken or disturbed as she passed the living room, all of the doors and windows shut and locked. Everything looked just the way she'd left it. Agnes distantly wondered if perhaps she'd hallucinated the crash in her fright.

But then he was in front of her, a large, hulking figure opening his arms as if waiting for a hug. Agnes screamed as the shadowed man quickly stomped toward her, backing her into a corner as she swung her scissors out wildly.

"Stay away!" she shrieked, but the man didn't hesitate, closing in on her with rapid, steady steps.

"Someone help!" Agnes screamed, as red lights began to flash all around her. "Help me!"

She woke to an empty house. Agnes was initially too stunned and confused to assess any damage, but once she did, it seemed like the intruder had done nothing at all. All around, everything seemed to be in order. No broken glass, no missing jewelry or appliances. There was no sign that anyone had even been there.

The phones were working again now, and the police were initially kind as they took her statement. "So he didn't take anything?" the officer asked as two others looked around. "Are you sure?"

"I don't see anything missing," Agnes said. "He just attacked me and left."

Or so she hoped. Fear lingered in the back of her mind that he was somehow still in the house, but the officers searched carefully and found nothing. It was like she'd dreamed the whole thing up.

"Well, let us know if anything does end up missing," the officer said, though his tone had changed. It sounded like he was talking to an alarmist old woman who'd wasted his time, not the victim of a break in. "Maybe you should stay with family for a few days."

Agnes didn't miss his change in tone, but she feigned ignorance regardless, hoping they'd take her seriously if the man appeared again.

Her nephew and his wife insisted she stay with them once they'd heard, and even if it was borne of condescension, the police officer wasn't out of bounds to suggest Agnes not be alone for a while. She packed a bag for the weekend, and soon she was settled at her nephew's place.

The ladies at the bridge club were a nervous, excited bunch when she told them what had happened. They had a million questions, alternating between prying, comforting, and sharing their own brushes with danger. A few expressed fear that the man may be out there, targeting elderly women. Agnes noted that she couldn't even be sure the figure had been a man. No features, no details, much to the disappointment of the ladies.

Though she had resolved to stay a while with her nephew, Agnes still needed to take care of her plants. She made a point to swing by before heading back for the evening. But when she returned to the house, something was different. She couldn't immediately put her finger on it, but it occurred to her after a moment that the paint along the walls had begun to flake, as if neglected over a long period of time. Agnes had just had the walls painted. It was odd that they looked so faded now. Too much direct sunlight, perhaps.

She closed the curtains.

For the next four days, very little changed in Agnes's routine, and she began to feel normal again. She discussed moving back into her home, much to the dismay of her nephew and his wife, who encouraged her to stay a little longer. But the ladies at bridge club were requesting her scones for the upcoming brunch, and Agnes never truly felt relaxed in any kitchen but her own. The merchant at the corner store had missed her when she'd failed to come in for several days. He tossed in a few free lemons for her scones, if she promised to bring him one.

Come evening, Agnes made dinner and listened to her records, the curtains firmly closed, though she didn't let her mind linger on why she'd been sure to close them. She was able to do her dishes in peace, and her bedtime was uneventful.

She woke before the sun had risen but found she couldn't sleep, so Agnes decided to make the scones early. While prepping the oven, she noticed some discoloration on the burners and leaned in for a better look. A scrape with her index finger revealed the marking to be rust. It was strange, like the flaking. Agnes had always taken pride in maintaining her home. Was it the air? Humidity? Was she going to have to replace her stove?

But when she turned from the oven to the sink, the man was there, his arms open as if to embrace her. He took quick steps to close the space between them before Agnes could respond with anything more than a scream. It was brighter this time, the light glowing overhead, yet she still could not see who this person was. Just shadows, no features — a silhouette of a person with a corporeal touch.

Agnes snatched a pan from the back burner and swung it at the intruder. It struck him and bounced back, the force knocking it from Agnes's hand. She tried to flee, but it grabbed her, squeezing her tight, harder and harder until she couldn't breathe. She could see her reflection in the steel door of the refrigerator, saw a woman much older than her, fighting for breath.

She woke on the living room floor and found it stained and dusty. The carpet looked worn and abused, nothing like the vibrant floral pattern she was used to. She was alone, like before, and it was morning.

This time, only one officer came.

"And nothing is missing," the officer clarified. "Like last time."

Agnes fretted about what this could mean. Another break-in, but no indication that anyone had been there or why. A nagging fear that this was all in her head lingered, but her body still hurt where she'd been grabbed. She was certain she'd bruise from the treatment.

The officer mentioned Adult Protective Services. Agnes agreed to stay with her nephew again.

"You can stay through the weekend," her nephew agreed, though his previous enthusiasm had dwindled slightly. "We have the extra room."

At bridge club, Agnes felt unable to connect as easily with the others, though they smiled and nodded at her when she spoke. Their conversations seemed guarded and foreign, something created only for them, to which Agnes was not invited. Even at the corner store on her way to water her plants, the merchant didn't seem particularly enthused to see her.

Back at the house, there was no mistaking the change in condition. The gutters were bowing, the roof missing a tile here and there. When had this happened? She'd been stopping by every day.

Inside, some of the wallpaper was peeling, and she noticed water stains had formed in several spots. Agnes frantically tried to find the source of any potential leak, but there was nothing. It was as if the house had simply been forgotten for many years, and she was coming back too late.

The sudden disrepair brought back the feelings from the previous day, when she'd started to doubt herself and what she was experiencing. She reached for the phone and found that tears were running down her face. It was too much. She had to deal with it now before it got worse, but she didn't even know where to start. What was happening to her home? To her? That stranger at night, would he be back? Would it ever be safe to sleep in her house again?

Agnes couldn't stand the sight of those stains on the wall. She turned and left through the front door, leaving the watering for another day.

Her nephew and his wife were quiet at dinner. Agnes fretted in the silence of the dining room. Every scrape of a fork or knife on ceramic sent her out of her skin.

That evening, Agnes dreamed of the shadowy intruder, saw him coming after her on a busy street as everyone around her passed by. She screamed for help but no one bothered to look as the stranger closed in on her once again.

In the morning, Agnes was too tired to bake anything for the ladies' brunch, so she drove out of her way to the corner market. The merchant was cold to her as he rang up three packages of chocolate chip cookies. He seemed relieved when she completed her purchase and left. The bridge club ladies disapproved of the cookies, but didn't say so. It was in their faces, the way they failed to even fake a smile. Some of them stared at Agnes and whispered amongst each other.

Agnes wanted to run and hide. She wanted to bury herself in the comfort of her home, but now she was afraid to even go there. The plants would die if she didn't, but she stayed in her car for a long while before forcing herself to go inside.

The bitter scent of rotting foliage struck her nose as soon as Agnes opened the door. She'd only missed a day, yet all of her plants had not only died, but started to decompose. Gnats buzzed about in the humidity of the house, the paint in the hallways clumping off in places, warped and discolored.

It was like the house had been left to decay for well over a decade. There was no other way to explain what it had become. The den was covered in dust and debris. In her room, the wallpaper stains had taken the shape of figures stretching along the plaster.

Agnes could stay only a few minutes before she burst into tears and fled to her car. Nothing made sense. Was she losing her grip on reality? Would other people see the house as she saw it? Maybe the police officer had been right to doubt her.

Agnes heavily contemplated talking to her nephew and seeking his help. She weighed it on her mind as she drove to his home, but when she arrived, she found him, along with his wife, waiting at the door.

"You've overstayed your welcome, Agnes," her nephew said. "I think it's time you go back home."

Agnes stood stunned, trying to find the words to explain what she'd been through. But her nephew and his wife remained unmoved, arms folded, eyes cold. It was like they were looking at a stranger, and even as she cried on their driveway, they didn't so much as flinch.

As she returned to her car, Agnes tried to think of where she could go. The women at the bridge club had all shut her out. She had no other family available, and it wasn't as if the police could do anything for her.

So Agnes drove home. With nowhere else to go, she had to return to her house and pray the intruder didn't come back. A part of her hoped that the damage had all been in her mind, that she'd open the door and find that her home was pristine as ever, even with all that that would entail.

She reached her block quickly and saw a few of her neighbors in their yards. Some of them looked at her as she drove by, but none of them smiled. In fact, they looked upset to see her, like she'd come to cause problems. Even as she parked, a neighbor and his children scowled at her, silently watching. Agnes kept her head down as she hurried inside, glancing over her shoulder to see the icy glares she could certainly *feel* at her back.

She opened the door to find that nothing inside had improved, and the smell had only intensified in her absence. The walls themselves were falling apart now, swollen from water damage. Agnes stumbled through the halls in muted horror, hand to her mouth as she took in the wreckage of her home.

A crash outside made Agnes run to the window, and for a moment, she thought she saw the intruder in the waning light. But no, she recognized this figure. One of her neighbors. And he'd brought others.

They were gathered around her car, and Agnes found herself unable to move from her spot, just watching to see what they did.

The crash echoed through the air once more as another neighbor brought a bat to her rear window, shattering it to the sound of cheers by the others. They were all armed, she realized, nausea gripping her and squeezing her throat. Bats, rakes, rocks. Bits of pipe. And they were destroying her car, dismantling it with every strike.

Agnes snapped out of her stupor and reached for the phone, but there was no dial tone. Just like that night, when the intruder had first entered her life. Only breathing. Wheezing.

Outside, the night lit up as they set her car ablaze. Their shadows danced across the driveway, stretched out like oily creatures surrounding their prey. Through the curtains, the growing embers looked like flashing lights. The neighbors celebrated and laughed, voices echoing in the night, until they stopped in unison and turned to face her.

Agnes stumbled back from the window. There was nowhere to go, and as she ran through the house to try to find shelter, Agnes realized the entire structure was completely dilapidated. She didn't recognize her home at all. She had tripped and fallen into a nightmare that only held the essence of her once safe space.

Agnes ran to her room and locked the door as if the decaying barrier could do anything to protect her. Everything around her was falling apart, mildewed and ruined, a mockery of the life she'd built and immortalized in this house. She recognized this place, yet she had never been here.

Straight across from her, there was something protruding from the wall, jagged beneath the paint like an infant against its mother's stretched belly. It drew her eye and, for a moment, all of her attention. There was something hidden here, in this festering skin and bones. Something important and terrible.

There were answers in these walls. All around, the rotting drywall cracked and crumbled, but the bulging section of the wall remained intact. It was the one thing that the house had preserved for her.

Agnes crossed and dropped to her knees, reaching out with shaking hands. When she touched the wall it gave way beneath her fingers, and she was able to dig into it like wet sand. She pulled away the sludge, wiping at the mulch and debris to reveal what lay beneath, and as she managed to create an opening, the rest of what was inside spilled out like entrails.

It took her only a moment to see what it was. Even in its current condition, she recognized her own body. Naked and partially decomposed, skin falling from bone, but her face clear and distinct.

Agnes put her hands to her own face and sobbed, the sound tightening with her strained vocal cords as the weeping turned to wailing.

Outside, the crowd had moved on from her car and was beating on the house from all sides. They smashed the walls with fists and weapons and anything they could grasp. The foundation could barely support itself, and she felt it giving way as if it were connected to her body.

Up above, the ceiling groaned. Agnes screamed along with it as the entire structure collapsed and swallowed her whole.

THE GIRL

by Carlin Dixon

The Girl awoke bleary-eyed like any other mundane day. Lazily rolling over in bed, she glimpsed the time: 9:30 am on a Tuesday. "Tuesday is a boring day," she said aloud to no one in particular. She began to wash her face, bored with the same monotonous routine. She felt empty, though whether that was from her lack of breakfast or just the usual emptiness within her she wasn't sure.

She wasn't unaccustomed to unpleasant feelings. That was her normal, she didn't know any different and thought nothing of it. Doesn't everyone feel this way? Her life often felt chaotic and full of commotion, in a constant state of panic and on her toes, unable to settle. She made a cup of tea and cuddled up in her housecoat to bring some warmth to herself. It had thus far been a particularly lengthy, bitter winter that had left her feeling bitter as a result. Even with the fireplace going in the living room, she couldn't shake the chill.

The morning dragged into the afternoon and 3:00 rolled around. Looking for a break in her day, she felt suddenly inspired to go for a walk and get a coffee at the nearby cafe. "At least it will get me out of the house," she thought, wrapping herself in her plush coat as she stepped out the door and felt the fresh chilled winter air hit her face.

She gulped the air and breathed in deeply, feeling its cleansing powers wash through her, rejuvenating and refreshing. Setting off briskly, she made her way towards the cafe on her standard route, taking in the usual sights and the familiar smells. As she walked, she noticed dog walkers, friends socializing, and a bluebird swooping overhead out of the corner of her eye. "Pretty bird," she thought to herself as she carried on.

Arriving at the cafe, she ordered the same coffee that she'd been getting all her life. "No use messing with a good thing," she reckoned as it always did the trick. As she stood waiting for her coffee, her mind wandered to far-off places and magical worlds she wished she could be a part of, and the heroes she wished she could befriend from stories she'd heard long ago. She thought of changes she hoped for in her own life, and wondered if the heroes in those stories would have as difficult a time enacting such change themselves.

The barista handed her the coffee. As the girl took the latte, she nearly spilt it all down the front of her jacket. "Oh, you absolute divvy! Real good job you fool," she furiously thought to herself. Embarrassed, she quickly thanked the barista and began to make her way back home. Not long after starting her route back, she came across a road closure that had seemed to appear in the time it took her to grab her coffee. "NO FOOT TRAFFIC! USE DETOUR ROUTE!" the rather angry-looking sign read. "Ugh!" she exclaimed. Not the sort of shake-up in her day she had hoped for.

She began following the detour route and was taken down streets and paths she had never ventured down before. Beginning to wonder where she was and if she'd ever make it back home, she noticed a community events board. Walking over to inspect for a closer look, a bright flowery poster caught her attention; "Community Garden plots: Register now for springtime." Intrigued by the notion, the girl grabbed a tab with information and tucked it into her pocket. "That could be fun," she thought, carrying on the detour route back to her house.

After what felt like ages of walking in circles, she finally arrived back at her house tired and ready to get back into her cozy housecoat. That outing had become much more than The Girl had bargained for and she was happy to be back. Sitting down in front of the television screen, she put on something to pass the time. As she sat there zoning out to a lighthearted show, she felt a wave of unpleasant feelings wash over her. "I want to go home," she suddenly cried. These words startled her, as she was in her house and by all accounts should be "home." Shaking her head, she disregarded her outburst and continued with her series, trying to get the evening over with so she could get to bed. She couldn't be bothered with anything more today and the emptiness inside her was becoming too much to bear on this particular evening.

Remembering her intrigue at the notion of the community garden, The Girl rooted the small paper tab out of her pocket. She went to the address on the slip of paper to fill out the form and registered her interest. "I mean, why not?" she thought, putting her phone back down. It immediately buzzed, and she picked up her phone surprised at such a quick response. "Congratulations!" it read, "You have been approved for your very own plot of land in the neighbourhood community garden." Delighted at the news, she did a little happy dance. Something to look forward to! How wonderful. That night she retired to bed enraptured by visions of flowers and potential blossoming in her mind.

SPRING:

It was a beautiful sunshiny day. Spring had sprung and the winter had melted away. The change of seasons brought with it a sense of hope and a feeling of fresh renewal, and new possibilities. The girl awoke to a message alerting her that her garden plot was ready for her. "Plot number 42 is waiting for you," the message read. She had almost forgotten about the garden entirely, so was thrilled at the reminder. "I'll go there right away!" she exclaimed gleefully, hopping out of bed, ready to start this new day of seemingly limitless opportunity.

After getting herself ready, packing her things and some tools, The Girl departed her house and made her way to the community garden. She arrived at the main garden gates and pulled up the map from her recent email guiding her to her new green space. Studying the map for a moment, she opened the garden gate and meandered down the path up the forest-covered hill, and over to plot 42. The plot was secluded, surrounded by large wise old trees; maples, oaks, willows, and pines. Here, there was nobody else but the woodland creatures. As she walked towards her new slice of land, the sweet scent of lilacs filled her nose. Looking around, she observed several stunning lilac trees dripping in little flowers of pink, purple, and white. Lilacs were her favourite flower, and she couldn't believe her luck that there were so many right there in her new plot of land.

Her attention turned to the garden bed next. It was raised, encased by wooden planks, filled with weeds and all sorts of things that she didn't believe belonged there. The Girl put her stuff down beside the garden bed, took a breath, and got to work clearing out the overgrown garden bed. "It must be perfect!" she thought to herself, frantically digging and pulling at the wild plants that had for some time made a home in her newly acquired plot of land. While she knew gardening magazines weren't going to be breaking down the door to snap photos of her space, she still held herself to the incredibly high standards one would expect from an award-winning garden. Besides, being busy at all times was a welcome distraction from whatever unauthorized thoughts and feelings may otherwise creep up inside her. So busy, busy, busy. She was like a little bee buzzing about the garden almost aimlessly. Never quite finishing the last task before starting up a new one.

The time ticked on, and her mind wandered as she worked away. Thoughts of deadlines, past social faux pas, and the opinions others might have of her clouded her mind in a swirl of negativity. The swirl grew into a tornado and was suddenly far too much to bear.

A bird nearby sang its call and startled her. Like being awoken from a trance, she fell away from the mind tornado and was shoved back into reality. She looked around and realized that, at some point, she had stopped tending to the garden and was now just kneeling in the dirt dozing off into space. "I want to go home," she cried as she picked herself up and stood looking around.

Her eyes darted through her surroundings in an attempt to identify the intruder that had frightened her and noticed the bird that had called to her. A bluebird was perched on the branch of a nearby willow tree looking at her quizzically. "Huh. And what are you looking at?" she muttered, gazing at the bird. She felt envious of the creature and its peaceful energy. "Oh, to be a bird in a willow tree on a beautiful day." She sighed. "But I am not a bird, I am a tired cranky girl who's had quite enough for today, and I want to go home." Grabbing her belongings, she set off towards the garden gate and back down the path.

After a long walk back to her house, she flung open the door, marched into her room and collapsed on the bed. Exhausted from the physical labour of the day, she felt her body ache for home and comfort, still unsatisfied despite being back in her bed. "What even is a home anyway?" she thought to herself. The Girl never really knew what the answer to that was. She concluded that it was a complicated answer to a complicated question, one that she was unlikely to solve.

SUMMER:

Summertime arrived and living was easy. It felt at once as though no time had passed at all, whilst simultaneously flying by. The Girl's days had become filled with tending to her garden, using every spare minute to visit and work away in her green space. She would eagerly await her chance to play with her plants, lovingly tend to her vegetable crops, enjoy her various flowers, such as lavender and sunflower, and get her hands into the earth. Pride was slowly but surely building within her, and as the garden flourished, she too felt a growing sense of accomplishment.

Over time, The Girl was able to begin shedding her perfectionist tendencies and ideas of the flawless garden. She let nature do what it pleased. It was easier to work with the prospering vegetation and flora rather than attempt to tame that which cannot be controlled. Perhaps it was the healing power of being in the sun and the dirt. Or perhaps it was the happy distraction from her previous cycle of negativity. She wasn't sure, but she was grateful for her garden, and all the new lessons about nature, herself, and life that she was learning every day she spent there.

The Girl delighted in experiencing daily changes as fresh greenery reached out with its new blossoms, sprouts, and leaves. She had even made new friends, as she became familiar with the wildlife in the garden. Sporadic visits from squirrels, snails, bunnies, and the occasional fox always brightened her day and gave her company while she worked. One friend, in particular, was a regular visitor, and she looked forward to the flap of wings overhead to alert her to the arrival of her guest.

The bluebird made a habit of perching on the willow branch nearby and watching as The Girl danced around her garden, pruning bits here and there. Truthfully, The Girl was always looking for something more to do in the garden. She enjoyed the sanctuary and peace of the forest around her and endeavoured to spend all her time there. Something was changing within her, and while she wasn't quite sure what, she knew she felt her best while in the garden.

Some days, she would bring a book and sit against the base of the willow tree, its branches cascading down around her, shielding her from the outside world. On other days, she would dance barefoot in the grass with flowers in her hair, feasting on strawberries from her garden as she moved about freely through the growing flowers. She truly was falling in love with this garden, all the moments it shared with her and the freedom it brought. Indulging in the smallest of delights such as the sun on her cheek or the summer breeze in her hair were some of the brightest moments in her day.

After a morning of digging about in the garden, The Girl lay on her back in the long sweet-scented grass, looking up at the scattered fluffy white clouds in the bright blue sky. The golden sun beamed down through the clouds and warmed her body, making her feel as though she were glowing from within and emanating warmth herself. The playful sounds of nearby squirrels chasing each other up the willow tree made her smile. "A jovial game can be made from anything if you wish it so, I suppose," she called over to the squirrels.

A loud whirring mechanical screech from nearby caught her attention, and she sat bolt upright to see what was going on. A groundskeeper was standing near the lilac bushes with a jarringly loud chainsaw beginning to hack away their beautiful limbs. "STOP!" she cried running over. "What are you doing?!" She shouted breathlessly.

"I'm just trimming them back you see. I was told to shape them to be more uniform, and tidy," explained the wrongdoer.

"But why?! They're perfect!" The Girl retorted using all the courage she could muster. "They don't need trimming, you can't control them, they're natural, and they will do what they like. Look, they aren't hurting anyone. Please leave them be."

The offender paused for a moment to consider her words. "I mean, I guess if they aren't buggin' you, I can leave these as they are. You sure you don't want me to trim them back? I do think they would look better."

"Thank you but there's no need for that! I'm quite happy with them as they are," explained The Girl. "I'm happy to take over anything that needs doing in this area myself! It's really no bother, and I'd much prefer to let them grow as they wish." She was becoming shaky. She hadn't expected such an intrusion on her magical sanctuary.

"Right, I'll leave 'em be, but let us know if you want anything cut back at all," the groundskeeper said, before turning and setting off back down the path.

Feeling small and deflated she retreated over to her garden bed, hurt and violated by the unwelcome surprise. She began to feel as though she was falling, spiralling downwards from atop a majestic mountain. Down, down, down to the very bottom. "I want to go home!" she sniffled, lip pouting and quivering.

The Girl gathered her things and made her way down the path, through the garden gate and back to her house. Once through the door, she got into bed and cried. She wanted to go home, to feel the safety and the comfort of a home, and it was still lacking. Something was missing, and she couldn't quite put her finger on it.

The emptiness she had felt many times before filled her once again and every terrible thought and feeling flooded back to her leaving her unable to think. "What even makes a home anyway?" she thought as she curled up under the bedsheets. She aspired to start anew the next day after a good night's kip. Looking sleepily through the open window, she saw the stars in the night sky. As she was gazing up at the stars and dreaming of an effortless tomorrow, she spotted a bird's nest in tree outside. "Oh, to be a bird," she thought, as she drifted off to sleep.

AUTUMN:

As summer to a close and the days grew shorter, her time spent in the garden remained unchanging as she was forever finding new ways to keep busy. Change was in the air and the smell of the garden made it her favourite place to be. Whether tending to it or creating something from its numerous gifts of crops and other treasures, there was always something to bring her back there. Much like her squirrel friends who were keeping busy preparing for the coming winter, she began to do the same. She preserved her harvest in all sorts of wonderful concoctions and gathered firewood getting ready for the cooler weather ahead.

She planted some autumn bulbs with the excited anticipation of how they would bloom come next spring. A sadness was building within her, and she dreaded the first snowfall. Very soon, she wouldn't be able to be in her garden all day. She had found a sanctuary where she felt safe and free and was worried about what her life might look like without it. She was dreading the idea of being trapped in her house all winter. Painful memories of the emptiness from previous years haunted her, making her uneasy. The house never really felt like home despite having all the things homes would realistically contain.

She sat in stillness for a moment, looking up at the trees and the golden afternoon sun shining down through the colourful autumn leaves. Inhaling a big breath of fresh air, she began to feel grounded.

A feeling that had only ever before been experienced in fleeting moments washed over her. It was too difficult to grasp, and she was unable to hold tightly. It was joyful, it was peaceful, and it was safe. This feeling she had been searching for all along, trying frantically to create and replicate her whole life was suddenly filling her like a warm glow in abundance. It almost startled her. She wasn't used to feeling this way and was unsure how to exist without commotion, chaos, and panic. It was unfamiliar, but the more she went with it, the more right it felt.

She knew then what the answer was. The answer to the question that was always nagging at the back of her mind for as long as she could remember. She knew that home was a place within herself, and it had been there all along. That loving herself unconditionally, forgiving herself, speaking kindly and investing in herself would build the walls of home around and within her, intertwined in her unique space of comfort and magic.

Once she tended to her inner garden with love, care, and compassion, she was able to watch the seeds of self-worth grow. Her garden flourished, blossomed, and grew with every kind thought, every act of caring and word of love she invested. She built her home within herself where she least expected it. When she stopped desperately searching, it came to her like a memory that had long been forgotten.

Nature had given her many wonderful gifts indeed. The lilacs taught her to enjoy the moment before it's gone, the sunflowers taught her strength, the woodland friends taught her acceptance, the lavender, a calmness, and the trees around her rang with teachings of longevity. All of these coming together to be her greatest Teacher.

The bluebird swooped in and perched on the willow tree. She looked up at her friend with misted eyes, grateful for all that she had and all she learned. The home she had always painfully yearned for, was now hers to keep and take with her wherever she pleased. She finally found it, her peace.

And she was home

WHOLE TIME

by David Simmons

Whole time, we know this guy from the Southside who drank so much lead growing up that now he can't die. Now that might sound counterintuitive, on account of the toxic metal exposure, but this motherfucker is impervious. Dense metaphyseal lines all through his long bones. They say he can't board a plane without causing a commotion.

"I could go raw in these hoes if I wanted to. The metal protects me. I don't have to use condoms. I *choose* to. The reason I use condoms: just because I can't get sick, doesn't mean that I can't get someone else sick. I would never do that. That's irresponsible."

That's what he always says. He's considerate in that way. And it's not just that he can't get sick.

We tried shooting him.

Last summer, we took him out back behind Damier's place and shot at him with Magnums and Glocks and AR's. The bullets just came to a stop and rolled down his chest, the sound of metal on metal twinkling. We guess he's mostly lead now—he must weigh a ton. We even tried to hit him with a car once, but it jacked up the car and for a while we had to Uber everywhere.

What if you could become something greater than yourself?

Damier says that men with pale faces and black holes for mouths ride in with the morning tide of rush hour traffic, snatching all the babies up. Would you believe that shit?

In the city, 2,200 children go missing every year. The majority of these missing children come from neighborhoods east of the River, obviously. These are crimes against Nature.

On the way to the FEMA building at 500 C Street, I passed by the Potomac Inn and heard somebody call my name. I looked up and saw Sheila, with her almond eyes and all that hair, waving at me from the sixth-story window.

"Hey, girl!" I waved back. "When did you get back?"

Sheila smiled. "Just last night. They gave me a chauffeur all the way back from the airport. They had free Fiji water bottles in the backseat. I took, like, six of them. They didn't even notice. You can have one if you want."

"Already. I'm on my way to FEMA to get that check, you feel me?"

Her eyes lit up. "Me too! My appointment is later today."

"I had my appointment with the Recovery Support Specialist last week," I told her, "where he informed me that I would be entitled to compensation."

I admit, I winked when I say the word *compensation*. What I didn't tell her, is that for what I got, they had to be giving me at least seven hundred a week. Shit, maybe a whole stack.

And like Damier always says: best *believe* I'm coming for that check.

Damier also says that if you go swimming in the Anacostia River, you come out of the water with superpowers. What Damier does *not* say, is that the majority of the time nobody gets any superpowers. Most times, they come out with their limbs melted off, flapping their new flippers like human-dolphin hybrids.

Whole time, you don't need religion to be inspired. Expressions of individuality can come from within. At first, we didn't know how to receive our blessings.

We were so small back then.

And yet, so was the mustard seed. With faith in ourselves, we can move mountains.

We see our idea of freedom in objects that we judge as beautiful. The degree of beauty is directly proportional to how much freedom we perceive in the object. The human desire to be free is universal—so are the objects we find beautiful.

Maybe our blessings were beautiful. Perhaps, they had the potential to be beautiful. But keeping them tied down, trapped underneath layers of clothing, was anything but freeing.

The thing about hope is that it impedes us. Hope for salvation dampens our appreciation for our current existence. Only by turning away from hope, can we ever begin to appreciate life. We must understand that we were pulled from the void, so there is no need to fear it. There is so much relief in acceptance.

We needed to accept our blessings.

We needed to let them free. We needed to become a part of nature. Through freedom, the city would see the beauty of our nature.

"**W**ell, maybe I'll see you later," Sheila said, and I hoped that when she said *maybe* she meant *maybe* as in: she hoped I would take the initiative to see her later.

I waved goodbye and kept walking to the FEMA building—tall and foreboding and made of black glass.

Inside the building, the investigator said, "As your advocate, I advise you to file an SI-60."

I asked her what the hell an SI-60 was.

She looked at me with a frog face.

I looked right back at her. "Ma'am, I'll have you know that I am a victim of contaminated drinking water. I believe the Washington Post referred to this shit as an epidemic, yes? All these toxic metals probably fried my brain. How the fuck am I supposed to know what an SI-whatever is?"

The investigator sighed and stared at her computer monitor. "You're a Ward 8 resident?"

"Yes."

"And you've been a Ward 8 resident for how long?"

"All my life. I was born in a basement on Good Hope Road. My Grandma's basement. She still lives there to this day."

"Uh-huh." She clicked away on her mouse, focused on whatever was on the screen.

"Whole time," I told her, "I know this fish—well, I don't exactly *know* this fish, like, personally or anything—but what had happened was, I went fishing this one time in the Anacostia River and hooked a big-ass catfish with a whole bunch of extra eyeballs. We pulled that fish out of that murky water and dropped all thirty-two pounds of channel cat onto the grassy bank. No fakin', it squawked like a bird. Maybe a seagull, or one of those nasty-ass Canada geese. You should write this down."

The investigator tapped away on her keyboard and the music being pumped out of her Bluetooth speaker was a cover of *Sweet Child O' Mine* by Guns N' Roses, performed by Sheryl Crow.

"I have to see the appendage," she told me, while taking out a digital camera. "It's the only way we can ensure that you receive your benefits package."

I lifted up my shirt and pushed.

The woman was a professional. She took a quick look, snapped a picture, then went right back to her keyboard, tapping away like everything was fine.

I sucked in air—retracted my appendage.

Before I put my shirt down, I asked the investigator for a paper towel to wipe off the plasma or sap or whatever it was.

Like Damier always says: I ain't finna stain my Lacoste for nobody, not even my goddamn self!

We propose to you the classical totems: the laurel branch, the myrtle bough and the ivy vine. The artist thinks, feels and plays. Play—represented by the ivy vine—is wild and feckless, and yet, it reconstitutes our potential. Sensuality—the myrtle bough—is tender, gentle. But Intellect—shown as the laurel branch—can tame play and encourage Sensuality to assert itself in a more productive manner.

Unlike the ancient Greeks, modern humans have a more developed sense of self. We are therefore more aware of our separation from Nature. We feel the natural, but we fail to feel naturally.

Our appendage—our blessing—gave us the spontaneity and Sensuality we would need to feel the heart of the city. To be *a part* of Nature, rather than *apart* from Nature. To grow in ways that we never thought possible. Our understanding of the city and its nature would tame it.

I was outside the building with my benefits card, trying to set up my login and password for the FEMA mobile app, when I saw Damier.

"My man, hundred grand!" he said, putting his hand out. I put out mine and we slid palms until our thumbs interlocked, the four fingers on each of our hands pointing straight out and flat.

"Damier, my boy. How you living?

He put flame to the end of a Newport   and shrugged. "I'm good," he said, blowing smoke out of one nostril. "How much they give you?"

"Three hundred a week, next twenty-five years," I lied. It's not like I could tell him the truth. When a motherfucker gets paid, everybody's best friend's sister's auntie's cousin wants to get paid too.

Like Damier always says: It be your *own* people.

He squinted at me suspiciously. "Three hundred a week ain't shit. How you only get three hundred when you got a whole appendage?"

I shrugged. "They say everybody got appendages now. Some fools even got two or three. Shit crazy."

"Boy, stop lying."

"Whatever."

I bummed a cigarette from Damier and headed back to the block. On 36th, I posted up on an abandoned rowhouse stoop and did some online shopping. I didn't have the FEMA money quite yet, so back then I was just filling my cart with the shit I wanted.

Almost everything we do is to avoid being dominated by the world around us. The rest of our energy is spent trying to look good. The children in the city have it the hardest. Without any education or resources, all they have is their youth and vitality. This is the only weapon they possess to avoid being dominated.

In *Notes From Underground,* Dostoyevsky says that the only reason people moan when they have a toothache is so they can lacerate the hearts of everyone around them. The individual knows that the moaning sounds won't alleviate his pain or improve his condition.

Because it's not about that. It's not about getting better. It's about making everybody else around you feel like shit.

Like Damier always says: you know how that schadenfreude be going!

Damier also says that pale-faced men in windowless, black vans from NIH, come down to the Southside and snatch people up, cut off their appendages and cauterize them right there, in the back of the damn van. We even know some folks, personally, who claim that this happened to them.

But these are the same type of people that make fraudulent claims in an attempt to finesse FEMA, even though they never had an appendage to begin with. These are the folks that fuck it up for the rest of us—the ones with real blessings.

As far as the men in the black vans go? They would need a motive, a reason for coming down to the Southside. What could an appendage be worth?

Like Damier always says: it don't make dollars if it don't make sense!

It's a play on the word *sense.*

The word *sense* is a double entendre for the word *cents,* as in *change,* like *money.* Damier says we should refrain from explaining the punchline to people because it exsanguinates the joke and makes it not funny anymore.

I was posted on Farragut Ave, daydreaming about a designer tactical vest with the Burberry nova check   logos printed all over it. In my dream, I was able to weave my appendage in and out of the compartments of the vest. In my dream, it was impossible to tell that I was different.

"Hey, you," a musical voice said, snapping me out of my daydream.

It was Sheila, with the almond eyes and all that hair, but this time, she wasn't in her window six stories above me. She was *here.* Finally here. Right on the block with me. I couldn't think of anything clever to say.

When she smiled at me, the way her smile looked sounded like the song "Les Fleurs" by Minnie Riperton. "You shouldn't hide it," she said.

She caught me off guard. "Hide what?"

"You know what."

My face was on fire.

"I have blessings too," Sheila said, taking off her denim jacket and placing it on my lap.

The skin under my eyes felt wet. "Blessings?"

Sheila smiled at me and the Minnie Riperton song started playing in my head again. She turned around and showed me.

Appendages—*two* of them!—just like mine. They hung down her back, pulsating rhythmically, each of them protruding from identical six-inch openings in her shoulder blades, perfectly symmetrical and wet with ichor.

"Why do you think they sent me back from NIH in a limo, dummy?" Sheila laughed at me, musical laughter like the part in *Les Fleurs* when Elsa Harris and Kitty Hayward come in with the backup singing, and it goes: *throw off your fears, let your heart beat freely at the sign that a new time is born.*

Something was happening to me.

Something new.

My appendage deployed, ripping open my shirt, snaking across the pavement, leaving a trail of sap behind it as it slinked over towards Sheila.

She smiled at me, bright white teeth and healthy gums, and Minnie Riperton singing about how *inside every man lives the seed of a flower* as Sheila's appendages were coiling around mine, leaving behind a glowing trail of discharge.

A crowd started to gather around us. "Freaks!" someone shouted.

Minnie Riperton sang: if he looks within, he finds beauty and power.

Then I felt my back open up.

There was a tugging sensation, then release. I watched a new appendage shoot out and ensnare the bystander that called us *freaks.* I felt pressure at the base of my spine as the new appendage wrapped itself around them, coating their body in glistening sap.

More appendages burst from Sheila's chest and shoulder blades, slithering around, searching for prey like the tentacles of a giant squid. I couldn't stop the tears from coming. We used our blessings to appeal to the hearts and minds of the crowd that gathered around us— wrapping our appendages around them and appropriating their bodies.

To the left of us, our laurel branches crept along the sidewalk like kudzu. To the right of us, our myrtle boughs and ivy vines climbed up the glass store fronts of the liquor store and beauty supply shops. We became beautiful, all of us, the beauty of the scene drawing others closer to the writhing mass of limbs that we had become, and as more people approached us, we sprouted new appendages and appropriated them too.

Whole time, we know this guy from the Southside who doesn't believe in the value of fiat currency.

"When the federal government got rid of the gold standard in the 1930s, it substituted its citizens as collateral for the country's debts by pledging each citizen's future earnings to foreign investors. That's why they always got your name in all caps on shit like birth certificates, social security cards, driver's licenses, and tax documents. If it's written in all caps, then it only represents the corporate identity *you*, not the flesh and blood *you*."

That's what he always says.

He likes to talk about how paper money is backed by nothing but a legislative statute and how the concept of money itself came to exist by individual actors solving the coincidence of *double wants*. His '93 bubble Caprice has a license plate that reads *Republic of North Carolina*.

"Noble Ellano Hunt El-Bey, Executive Trustee for the Private Contract Trust known as ELLANO HUNT," he says. "That's how I sign all my shit. One may also use red ink, or add their thumbprint to documents, to avoid inadvertent submission. If one were so inclined."

We used to think he was an idiot. Now we are not so sure. What value could paper money hold for us now?

We had become something greater than what we were when there was only one of us. Staring into Sheila's eyes—which are now our eyes too—going on three days now without food or water, or the idea that we even need food or water anymore, and we are starting to think that fiat money isn't as important as we once thought.

Before we became a part of nature, we were obsessed with designer tactical vests. Not only were they a fashion trend—Damier had one with the Louis Vuitton logo printed all over it like the one Nick Cannon wore on Wild'n Out—but with a little imagination and DIY, we believed we could keep our first appendage completely concealed. The way we saw it, we'd cut out the bottom of the various vest compartments—the ones that the police put their magazines in—then weave our first appendage in and out through the bottoms and tops of the compartments until we ran out of compartments, and then, we could just tuck the rest of it up under the actual vest, or even over our shoulder, then wedge the rest under the shoulder strap part, so that the fabric covered the length and the thickness of it.

We wouldn't have to hold our breath in and clench all the time. It was the perfect solution.

All we wanted to do was hide!

Back then, we were still separated from Nature, hiding our radiant blessings from the world. We were ashamed of it, so it filled us. Pressing against our ribs, pushing aside our lungs and heart. It is impossible to contain beauty of that kind. Beauty of that nature demands absolute freedom. We had to stop fighting.

Now we do not hide our blessings. We have no compulsion to chase money and stack paper and blow it all on fashion trends. In nature, money is meaningless. We know that now.

We are the next stage of Evolution.

Damier always says: you gotta chase the bag at all costs!

When he says this, *chase the bag* is a colloquialism which means that one should pursue any and all opportunities for financial gain.

As we continue to appropriate the bodies of the city, soon, he too, will understand that chasing the bag is unnecessary.

CALLOUSED

by K.A. Wiggins

chew the callous on my left ring finger while my manager scatters soil across the sheets. The hotel knew my requirements. Half the world knows.

He apologizes. I switch to the index, testing the edges. Finding that point where numbness gives way. But steel strings have cut deep, and often. It takes more than teeth to score the skin now.

I'll move to the softer flesh on the inside of my arms later, after he leaves. Not that it'll help me sleep, not even with earth now properly ground into the linens. I've lost that sweet, lingering exhaustion. Hunger will keep me up until the next show, next stadium, next city.

I crawl between the sheets anyway, curling against coarse, cool dampness. It's the closest I can get to that half-remembered nest. It's the closest I can get to home.

I t's the duvets as get you.

No time for rolling out gentle when you've a dozen rooms to turn over before noon. Match corners, pinch, snap, tuck, and move on to the next, ignoring the aching in your back that'll turn to stabbing before the day's done.

First two weeks after school let out was always worst. Sweeping away dew-damp shreds of cigarettes from the patio at dawn, stripping beds and hoovering stairs right after, with a couple hours to catch my breath before heading back to scrub pots until midnight approached. Between shifts, and after, couldn't do much more than lay flat and grit my teeth against the hurt.

Whiskey helped. The hangovers didn't.

But it kept us going after da got bit by the wrong tick, lost his place, and started spending all he could get escaping his worn-out self. In a way, it was better after that for me, if worse for everyone else he couldn't remember not to strike out at. Him out the house forced me out, too, and earning my own way quick.

Once, poor fisherman's kids ate langoustines for school lunch 'round here and felt it a hard lot. But fresh seafood was for the holidayers by the time I came along, and the only time my gnawing emptiness eased was when I could bury it under the stolid weight of overdone and hastily devoured staff meals, before the dishes from evening service started pouring in. But though filling my belly helped, it never really stopped the hunger.

There's a special kind of horror to knowing there's something you need that you'll never get enough of. Never even get a proper taste of. And that hunger for *more* grew, until one summer, there was nothing ahead for me but the kind of work as turns you old and withered early, with naught to look forward to but half-remembered nights drinking to forget instead of doing what I was made for: fingers that craved the strings, coppery tang of the mic at my lips, feet stomping that scant patch of cleared boards in place of a stage But not even the roughest pub in town would so much as let me through the doors for a midweek set after da got us both banned for life.

So I spent the whole of that last summer planning my escape. And, when the nights grew longer, up I went into the hills with a battered case in hand.

The crowd is thin tonight—too thin. There's talk of cancelling dates, slowing the pace, trading shows for more press stops. It's all going online now anyway, my manager says, with more blustering optimism than business sense.

I tell him to rebook at smaller venues. Better a packed club than a half-empty stadium. Better a live crowd than a cold screen.

He babbles about positioning and appearances and fees. I wander off before he's done. He's in it for the money, but he has plenty—his cut, and most of mine as well.

Could do something about that. I remember what it was to care, if only just. But it's the music I can't sleep without. And the bigger the crowd, the wilder the energy, the better I feel.

I haven't been feeling great lately.

Four pubs and not a charity shop in the town that time forgot, but no bother; you could get anything in the post, even then. I stuffed that tiny wireless speaker under the bracken right quick, wary of the creeping brush of too many legs. You wouldn't believe the size spiders could grow to out here on the remote fringes of civilization.

I wasn't half bad as a musician, but if I'd been good enough to draw the gentry's attention, I'd not have needed to seek out a ring on the top of a hill at dusk. Themselves are known to like pretty things, talented things and, on occasion, foolish things. No beauty, nor yet world-class talent, but I'd not regret what smarts I had so long as I could pull one over on The Good Neighbours.

In truth, I'd've sold my very soul to make it. Not that Themselves needed to know that. But leaving wasn't the trick; it was arriving somewhere worth being that I couldn't seem to manage on my own.

The perfect track, the one that would change my future, was the best thing I'd ever heard. I loathed that transcendent voice with awe-fuelled bitterness even as I stole it for my own. I didn't need to be her to become her, not so long as The Good Neighbours were as far behind the times—and the technology of the day—as I'd been led to believe.

And then it was time. The distant islands were dark silhouettes against a fading sky. I moved to the music swelling from that tiny speaker as if it were my own, let it crawl inside my skin and out my fingers—and ignored pinpricks of pain as midges swarmed.

Aching vibrato faded into stillness. Sweat turned to shivers, twilight to night, and no one came.

I scrubbed at my damp face and shoved back at the pit opening inside me. It wasn't over. I'd try again at midnight, at dawn, every hour between. Or—maybe if I went to the shoreline? Maybe down in the trees, or the ruins of a cleared village, or—

And then, between one breath and the next, the earth opened for me.

I sleep in the back of a van—the middling-new kind, hardly a scrap of true metal to send my flesh buzzing. Saves spreading my meagre handful of dirt every night, making up my bed in pale mimicry of the one I dream of . . . and then scraping those precious grains together in the morning, legging it before some poor housekeeping wretch finds the mess I've made.

Saves other things, too.

Stadiums are a distant memory. Even the raw, ragged clubs are lost in the cracked rear view. Now I wander back roads to play to a straggle of regulars in bars and pubs and the odd community hall when fortune smiles, bearing down on worn fingerboards and thinning strings with fingers thick and dull.

I can't feel their eyes, their attention, their hunger. And I can't blame them—I can hardly feel the sway of the music myself anymore. But every so often, for a few magical beats—a buzzing, humming, glorious refrain, a sparkling, slicing, devastating song—the sparse crowd leans in, nods along, even dances. Those are the nights I can eat. And sleep.

Other times, they hunch against the noise. Or throw things.

I don't notice the bruises. I'm too tired. Almost as tired as when I started out.

I gave Themselves a twelvemonth of service in return for a life worth living, careful not to thank the gentry for their sharp-edged gift. If they recognized my trickery, they never made their displeasure known. Not for that, anyway.

Their land is a place of beautiful terror and painful wonder, and though there is little I may now speak of, the memories are consuming. As was the temptation to turn my course and abandon all resistance to their wicked and lovely ways.

But the gentry are not human. And though I cared nothing for my humanity and a great deal for what The Good Neighbours could give me, I would not be lured and changed. Instead, I wound myself tight around a core of yearning, learned much, experienced more, and clung to my dreams all the while. I nested in my hurtful cocoon and waited for the day I would transmute suffering into glory and emerge a creature remade.

And so, a year and a day after Themselves took me under the hill, I found myself once more amidst the bracken with bruised limbs and bleeding fingers clenched around a hastily clawed souvenir, raw and new and too spent to lift my head.

Still, when the sun rose and the dew began to lift, I turned from the sea, hitched a lift inland, and staggered into the first pub I came to. The rest happened fast, most of it public record, what with the interviews and the documentaries and that dreadful film.

I came back different—and the world fell in love.

It's easy to be beautiful when you're talented, and wealth follows after. True wealth—all the way fullness, bursting with the crowd's energy and attention and adoration, their hunger for the music stirring and filling and stoking mine night after night. My fingers danced and my voice soared, and I thought I had flown away from the hunger and the dull heaviness of my old life for good.

But then, all too soon, the world moved on. Delicious strangeness gave way to dull familiarity. Imitators siphoned off fans. Protesters soured the studios and bookings agents and venues against me.

Too dark, too fast, too much. It had to be wrong. *I* had to be.

The ending of my dream took longer than the starting, a lingering descent into obscurity and starvation; the death of one meteoric career helped along by the failing of an entire industry; a single star's implosion swallowed in the unwinding of a galaxy.

I was never one to sit back and accept my place for long. I earned these scars, toughened this hide, tore through the blisters and kept right on going until each fingertip was honed beyond feeling.

But now I'm alone. And I'm hungry. And I'm wondering: where did it all go wrong? When should I have stepped back from the mic, turned from the stage and known my place?

Would it have been better to climb out of obscurity on my own? Or rather, would it have been better to accept the drudgery of my small life? To keep that early ache, that pain, in place of this dreadful, sucking numbness?

It's late morning. I knock at another nameless pub in another nameless town in search of another nameless crowd—and for the first time, I don't know if I'll ask for a gig singing for my dinner, or just scrubbing pots.

And when the door opens, I can't even get the words out, because I know—I *know*—that's a lie. Whatever the ask, whatever the answer, it won't be enough. Because I knew what I wanted, and I did what I had to get it. And I'd do it all again in a heartbeat.

And that's the truth: I've *always* known what I wanted. It's time to take it back.

So I turn around and walk until I reach the nearest shore, with a pinch of soil in my fist to call me home. And I keep walking, as the waves lap against my toes, my knees, my chin, right out of this world and into another, where I can sing until my voice is raw and play until my fingers bleed and keep right on, because callouses never form in the Undying Lands—and Themselves are just as hungry as I am.

CONDEMNED

by Koji A. Dae

Mama and I are elbow deep in half-peeled potatoes when a sharp knock startles Mama, and the paring knife slips into the meat of her thumb. She sucks at the spot of red and snaps at me to go see who's there.

A human in a button-up shirt and jeans stares at me with hard brown eyes. My hands fly to my ears, trying to cover their points. Doesn't matter. He knows what I am. I don't say anything, so he won't get a peek at my sharp teeth.

He shoves a sealed envelope into my hands.

I hold it in front of my mouth. "Thanks?"

He grunts and takes out an electronic signature pad. I sign a squiggly mess on the slick surface, which he'll probably use to support the idea that we're all illiterate. I try not to care what they think, but when I close the door, I'm shaking like a leaf, tender and ready to fall.

When I lay the envelope on the table, Mama sniffs and juts her chin at it. "Well, open it."

I tear the edge and slide a single piece of paper from the envelope.

"Condemnation Order," I murmur and skim the jumble of numbers in the first paragraphs. "... illegally constructed and unsuitable for habitation... the house will be demolished... final notice to vacate the property."

Mama sinks into a chair, her thick eyebrows drawn close together. "Condemned?"

The word holds awe and hate, swirling like oil and vinegar. Our house isn't like the shacks on the edge of town. It was built properly by Mama's Grandfather. It's our home.

"What are we going to do?" I ask.

She takes her thumb from her mouth and wipes it on the apron. "Leave it to me."

I leave it to her, but five days later Papa is drunk in one of the seedy pubs that serve our kind, so long as we have money. When he's sober, he says he's fulfilling their expectations. Greenies are all drunks. Useless. Don't even try to integrate with the humans. Funny thing, he never drank before the order came. He was a hardworking man who pieced together enough money to keep my family fed and my ever-sprouting brothers clothed. But that letter broke something inside him. I haven't seen more than shadows of him in days.

Mama spends all her time at the courthouse, waiting in lines, filing papers, begging to speak with people who don't want her to exist. She comes home exhausted and hopeless.

One night I find Mama alone in her room, sitting on her bed, holding the bright green malachite pendant Gram left to her.

"Are you going to use it?" I ask.

"I can't do that." She doesn't even snap at me. She's that defeated. "The necklace is for balancing the City and the Forest. If I used it to save our house, I'd become exactly what the humans think I am."

"What's it matter what they think?" I harbor enough anger for both of us. "Might as well give them a reason to hate us."

She sighs and shakes her head. "It matters."

I sink beside her and take the pendant. It's cold, and I'm quickly lost in the swirling greens. Light here, dark there, a sparkle and shadow chasing each other. "Gram would have used it."

She curls up in bed and closes her eyes. "Maybe. But Gram isn't here, is she?"

It takes the city six men, two excavators, and less than an hour to demolish a house that has sheltered my family for four generations. It comes down clean, which probably surprises the human neighbors poking their heads from behind drawn curtains. Shouldn't a greenie house give off puffs of dirt while rats scurry from it? As if. Mother would have pulled our pointed ears if we tracked in the least bit of dirt.

I watch from the schoolyard where they can see me, hoping they feel a bit of guilt as I stand alone on the asphalt, the fall air curling around me with the warmth of decay.

Papa's still getting drunk. My brothers have been placed with our aunt. And Mama? I haven't seen her in days.

The excavators continue their strange ballet, pushing piles of brick to one side, wood to another. It surprises me how deft they are for such clunky machines, like Gram splitting out wool to spin protective charms.

I pull my threadbare cardigan tight and cross my arms over my stomach.

"Mara!" Mrs. Brightly calls from the corner. "You shouldn't be here, child."

Her tone holds both warning and a sliver of sympathy. I used to play with her daughter, Alexa. But when I started getting my wrinkles, she stopped letting us hang out. Didn't matter that me and Alexa spent hours examining our skin for a difference in color. I only took up the slightest tint of green when I stayed in the sun all summer, but I still had the ears. The high cheekbones. The tight mouth and sharp teeth.

Mrs. Brightly still says hello in passing, but she doesn't let Alexa talk to me.

I wave to her because I don't trust myself to say anything. Then I see a flicker of movement in the tree behind her and realize I'm not the only one who came. At least one of my brothers made it.

When the men finish, they pack up their tools and drive their excavators down the street in a macabre parade. I want to rush to the pile of memories before me, but I remain rooted to the asphalt, surprised by how small the house has been condensed. The waste of two storeys is shorter than a fifteen-year-old girl.

"Dingo, that you?" I call to the canopy of the oak tree.

The orange leaves shake, a few red ones fluttering to the ground, and then two sets of feet appear, followed by two skinny torsos and the shaggy, unkempt heads of my two brothers. Dingo runs to me and throws his arms around my waist, squeezing me tight. Darius keeps his distance. He's eleven now, supposed to be a man about these things. I reach out and grab him by his shirt, pulling him to me and Dingo.

We hold each other like that as the golden light fades to dark blue. "Things okay with Auntie Vivi?"

Dingo nods, but Darius kicks at the ground. "There's no room. And it stinks."

I pinch Darius' shoulder. It isn't her fault there are now twelve bodies crammed into her three rooms. "You be grateful she took you in. Help her as much as you can."

"Where you staying, Mara?"

That is the question. Auntie Vivi would take the boys. But me? No way. Humans think greenies all have the power. Greenies know it's just the women. And the women know their simple spells to grow gardens pale next to the control my family gets over the forest roots. Human or greenie — they're all afraid of power.

I give a weak smile. "I have a friend I'm staying with."

Darius rolls his eyes. He knows I don't have any friends. The truth? I'm looking for Mama. We need her.

I give Dingo a tighter squeeze. "You be good and listen. Okay?"

Then they're gone and I'm alone again. It's night, and I don't have a house to return to. I turn and walk up the steep hill that will take me into the woods.

The trees shut out the moonlight. I usually avoid the woods. Don't want to start rumors. Now I'm tripping over roots and stumbling through bushes, making a mockery of the heritage I've tried so desperately to deny.

I don't know where to look for Mama or why I even think she's here. Maybe she's with Papa, finding oblivion. But no, the women in our family have too much responsibility etched into our wrinkly skin to run away. I call out softly. My voice echoes around the tree trunks in an eerie whistle and the forest birds go silent. I'm afraid to try again.

My eyes finally adjust to the darkness, and I stoop low, looking for a flash of silver or white or gray. Mushrooms are supposed to be visible in even the dimmest light. I find a small one, poking its glistening cap from under a pile of decaying leaves. I drop to my knees, cup my hands around the small fungus and blow a slow, steady breath over it. I inhale, waiting.

Nothing happens.

I clench my jaw, swallow to calm my frustration, and try again.

This time a light tugging pulls at my hands, as if they're sinking into the earth. I breathe again and feel the microscopic tendrils of the mushroom and the strength of its family. Its connectedness provokes a pang of jealousy in me, and I almost snatch my hands away. But I need this shroom and its unending family.

I can't see through their network, but I can feel where the woods are cool and wet, where they are warm and dry, where the wind blows, where a deer has bedded down. And there. Where my mother curls against a tree with a strange jerking motion. Mushrooms know nothing of tears, but I know she must be sobbing.

I follow the network, touching other mushrooms briefly to make sure I'm on the right path. Then I no longer need them. Mama's hoarse voice bounces off rocks and trees, leading me to her.

She sucks snot into her nose and wipes dirt across her cheek, smearing tears rather than clearing them. "You came."

"You left."

She bites her lip and looks away. Her skin is darker than I've ever seen it. Her long hair hangs loose down her back with leaves and moss snagged in it.

"Have you been here this whole time?" I ask.

She nods. "I came to ask your Gram what I should do."

She should have stopped them. Saved our house. Our family. I swallow all that and say, "It doesn't matter anymore. They did it."

Her head falls into her hands and the sobs start again and it's no use talking to her, so I drop to my knees, wrap an arm around her, and put my head on her shoulder. I coo to her like she's the child.

"The necklace," she whispers. "I left it in the house."

Anger flares in me again. How could she be so stupid?

"I thought I would figure things out and come back. But everywhere I asked, it was the same. We can't use the magic for ourselves."

"Yeah, well if the woods want us to protect them, maybe they should start protecting us." I kick at a mushroom and its cap flies off its stem. Its pain makes me wince, but I don't care.

"It isn't that simple, Mara." Mama's collecting herself. Her nose is almost dry, and her speech is soothing again. "Gram found the balance between humans and our kind, but I never could. If the humans keep pushing into the woods..." She smooths my hair back and cocks her head to one side. Her eyes narrow, and she nods.

"No. The power only passes down when the previous matron..."

She kisses my brow. "You need to find your Gram's necklace. Find that balance and hold it. You need to be stronger than me."

I spend three days hating Mama. I don't go back to the woods, afraid I'll feel her decomposition. I sleep curled around trees in the park, hoping I blend in enough that no one will bother me. It's getting colder every night, and I shudder more than I sleep.

Darius finds me on the fourth morning and kicks my frozen feet. My toes scream with tingles and I curse at him. He laughs, ever the brother. "You want a coffee?"

I manage to sit up, and he pulls me to standing. We walk to a coffee machine at the edge of the park and he puts in some coins, ups the sugar to the highest level, and presses the button for a chocolate coffee. He knows I need the calories. He's too young to know that.

My stomach churns as hot liquid pours into the cup.

"Where'd you get money?"

"Don't ask," he grumbles.

I don't. It's either something embarrassing or illegal, neither of which our family would stoop to before. He pulls the paper cup from the machine and shoves it into my hands. It warms my fingers immediately. "How are you guys?"

He shrugs and kicks at a rock. "It's okay. Auntie Vivi acts like we're her own kids. Ain't nothing great about that, but it could be worse."

I don't know what else to say, so I sip the hot drink, letting it warm me from the inside.

Darius says, "I hear they're going to clear the house tomorrow."

"You been picking it over?"

He shakes his head. "Auntie Vivi won't let anyone near it. Says it's cursed."

Of course. Maybe she's right. This responsibility is nothing but a curse.

Suddenly his arms are around my waist and I barely have time to move the coffee away before his head crashes against my chest. He feels very much like a little boy again. "Take care of yourself, Mara."

Then he's gone, and my coffee is already cold.

I can't decide whether to visit the rubble under the cloak of night or in the safety of day. I don't want people to see me poking at trash — not that a broken house is trash, they just think anything I poke at must be. But if I'm discovered at night, they'll think I'm up to no good, and then it's a week in jail while they sort things out, and maybe a month if they pin something on me. Definitely a month. Best to go during the day. Around eleven o'clock. People will be at work, morning coffee break is over, lunch hasn't started. No one should be around to pay too much attention to me.

I wish I could put it off. Another week, day, hour... but soon there won't be any rubble to dig through, and I have to get Gram's necklace. Mama's necklace. Mine, now.

An old man sits in front of the apartment building. I recognize the curve of his nose and the large mole on his left cheek. I can remember the slightly sour, unwashed scent he carries in winter, especially since his wife died. As I approach the tumble of brick and wood beams, the man eyes me suspiciously. Like he's never seen me. It's not true.

We've passed each other almost every day. He's yelled at my brothers to be quiet when they played. To respect the neighborhood. Their elders. Him. And yet, it is true. His eyes have always glossed over me, like I was a placeholder instead of a person. He doesn't challenge me for being here, but he stares, finally interested in me.

I turn from him to the house. Or what was the house. It's hard not to see it as still standing — the faded shutters and exposed brick that welcomed me home every day. My feet carry me to where the front door should be, as if that's the only place I could possibly enter this pile. I trace over the threshold and down the main hall, past the kitchen where I can almost see Mama and me sitting at the table, sipping coffee.

I continue to my room. It was a luxury in the house, having a bedroom to myself. It was more luck than love, being the only girl. Three boys in one room, two in another. But I got privacy. I also got a hell-load of responsibility, looking after all those young boys.

My parent's room was directly above mine, and now they've tumbled together as if I never had anything of my own. The belongings we weren't able to get out in time are buried somewhere under this mess — the things we triaged as unimportant. And apparently Gram's necklace.

I squat and pick up a brick. It's heavier than I expect, and I swallow a grunt as I heave it to the side. It doesn't fly as far as I meant it to, and I'll just have to move it again. I need to be more careful. I don't have the energy or time to move the entire house twice. I pick my way to where I think my parents' bed would be and start digging.

By noon I'm sweating so bad I have to take off my cardigan and think about shedding my long sleeve shirt, but I expect that old man is still watching me, and I can feel other eyes, too. I don't need to show more skin to these people. They've seen my house gutted, that's enough secrets for a lifetime.

There's a considerable divot in the brick. I've started coming across the top of furniture. My mother's vanity, only mostly crushed. My dresser, somehow still standing. The dollhouse Grandpa made — pulverized, but the rag dolls intact. It's been years since I played with dolls. I used to take them into the yard, pretending I had sisters instead of brothers. Someone to share the burden of being a girl. Someone to play with.

One of the wooden beams is in my way. It's as thick as I am round, and twice as tall as me. The city said our house was rotting. If it was in such bad shape, shouldn't it have turned to dust when they sent their wolves to blow it down? There's no point in trying to move the beam, but I strain to lift it, anyway. To prove a point. All it proves is that this house is still stronger than me.

The strain brings tears to my eyes. I wipe them away, not wanting the neighbors to see me cry. My face must look like Mama's had before she... gave her power to me. I abandon the beam and move a smaller chunk of wood. Beneath it is the bright red of Mama's end table, splintered into pieces. I dig through them, my fingers bleeding and numb from the day's work. But within the shards I feel a cool chain of metal. I tug on it and a large pendant works its way loose from the rubble. Its green malachite glimmers in the sunlight. It's not even scratched — not the stone, not the setting, not the chain. Of course, the forest can't be hurt. Our entire family can be separated and destroyed, but not the forest.

I clutch the necklace and fall to my knees, scraping against the edge of a brick. Blood comes through my jeans, but I'm beyond caring. I sob like Mama did and hold the damned necklace to my chest, hating it and needing it at the same time.

"Hey, greenie, what you doing there?" The gruff voice pulls me from my grief and I sniff snot into my nose, trying to compose myself.

It's the old man in the apartment building. *Greenie.* He doesn't even know my name.

"It's my house!" I shout back at him.

"That house was illegally built on city land. Human land. You greenies are a bunch of thieves," he snarls at me, still full of hate when he's so clearly won.

I want to shout back that the entire city is built on our forest, but instead I clench the pendant hard in my hand. The setting digs into my palm, but I press harder and take a deep breath. I feel the entirety of the forest in the stone. Not just the mushroom network, but the trees. The animals. The soft decay and new growth. I feel its circular nature, nipping at the edges of town, trying to spread to its full glory. And I feel the buildings fighting back, standing strong, demanding their space.

Is this the power Gram felt? The one Mama wouldn't use? I sink deeper into it, closing my eyes against the glower of the old man. I feel the rubble of my house, my body growing in it like a sprout — a piece of the forest cast into humanity like forsaken spores.

Well, a mother who abandons her children has no say over how we grow.

I grit my sharp teeth together and reach within myself for the apartment beside me. I want to bring it down with a single shiver, but I don't have that kind of power. Yet. What I do have is enough to make the roots grow stronger until they crack the foundation. Years from now, the building will crumble. The humans will know what it feels like to be condemned.

THIS FRONTIER LAND

by Karin Hedetniemi

She never really thought about the kind of life she'd be living. Not having furniture or towels or money she'd need to pay people to do the things she didn't know how to do.

What would happen when the kitchen faucet broke and started gushing water on Friday afternoon of a holiday weekend. When the maintenance manager wouldn't be answering his phone. How water would be spilling all over the floor, and all she could do was keep yanking on the rusted shut-off valve, keep phoning the maintenance guy, keep mopping the floor with clothes from her suitcase because she didn't have any towels yet.

She never thought there'd be such loud fights through the walls. Sudden thumps of crashing chairs. Doors slamming. Threatening, unintelligible voices. The sound of someone grabbing a bag and dumping it over the table, taking their keys and credit cards and every last bit of change. Strange smoke coming through the vents.

She heard angry bottles rattling in that other sink, which is probably why her faucet broke. All that rage travelled through the pipes and had to burst out somewhere.

She never thought about who would help the boys with their homework on nights she wasn't there. But she thought endlessly about the sound of them eating cereal in the mornings—their sleepy pours, dribbling milk on the table, licking it up with their tongues. Their goofy faces reading cartoons on the back of the box.

These thoughts nearly drowned her when she climbed into the bathtub with all the wet clothes, sobbing until she couldn't breathe. Suffocating at not being able to hear their happy little slurps and chews and swallows, drinking the last of the sugary milk from the bottom of their bowls.

She felt pain in the middle of her chest, the bottom of her feet, and inside every tiny cell of her body, because she didn't know if the boys were still awake or fast asleep. She didn't know if their father was checking on them and gently taking their comics away and wishing them good night, or if he was watching their rosy-cheeked faces while they slept and dreamed.

Oh, how she wanted to be the one watching them dream. All the nights, all the dreams.

She kept revisiting over and over, the sounds of a thousand small cracks—each time louder, wider, closer—her body recording them like a seismograph tuned into signs of the earth splitting. Tuned into the future coming fast: that dark headlong train. She'd felt herself leaning over the edge of a precipice. She had to stop the train, stop the earth from splitting. There was no time left. She'd closed her eyes and jumped down inside another world—the old one instantly collapsing behind.

Now she was here in this unexplored Frontier Land. The one with broken pipes, no oxygen, but her boys left sleeping in the other world, protected in their dream nest, safe and warm. The only thing that made the impossible sacrifice, possible. The only thing that made it possible to breathe in a place without oxygen. Just desperation or the bravest love—impossible to choose.

Impossible to break down the courage of a choice. But slowing hanging up the wet clothes, finally hearing the phone ring, a realization spread through her thoughts like warm honey and cleared away the dark.

What made it possible was both. She was here now, in this Frontier Land, and the only ground to walk was forward.

NEW ME

by Em Dupre

I am arcing through space, the lights from distant stars smear across the sky in alien configurations. It is difficult to recall a time when the night did not unfurl in a brilliant array of colors and a matte black emptiness was all my inferior human eyes could see. I search my mnemonic storage for an example. My recollections of the night sky are few, glimpses here and there, used as a dark backdrop to other unfolding dramas. The rest of the data I must have archived. To mimic my former sight, I lower my optics and the spectrum of refracted particles fade, coalescing on the edges of my vision like a distortion of dreams. This new me can never quite get it right.

Even after all this time, some residual part still clings determinedly to my core, and aches where my heart used to be. *I retrieve more data* I am once again overwhelmed by the vividness, the clarity. It feels so real. These emotions in binary. For an instant I am completely human once again, residing in the hard, familiar body of a man.

*P*rocess.

The straining heater could not break the lingering hold of winter's grasp, panting air barely warmer than the outside. Twilight watched us drive on the nearly deserted highway. Going to the cabin was my idea.

I could almost feel the rigid steering wheel resting lightly in my hand. *Delete.*

See the gritty asphalt of the damp road curving slowly before us. *Delete.*

Hear the sticky gripping of the leather as I shifted in my seat. *Delete.*

Smell the fading coconut on her skin. *Save.* On her hair. *Save.* On my lips from when she kissed me earlier. *Save.*

My tongue tastes the sweetness her traces left behind in my memories. *Save.*

We passed the darkening silhouettes of trees that lined the highway as Jen crooned along to a beach rock song, in a key that would set dogs to howling. Rocking on its eighteen wheels, a truck lumbered closely in the next lane. *Pause.*

"Hey, I was listening to that", she protested when I fiddled with the dial.

"I was afraid The Ambassadors would pick up your singing and see it as an act of war. Look! Here they come now." I pointed through the windshield at the barren sky. Bad joke. *Delete.*

She hit me with that high beam smile and then let out an unrestrained laugh. Her curls would tumble as she threw back her head. Face upturned, her eyes would close. It killed me every time.

Using the rearview mirror, I met my eyes in the reflection and felt fear curdle the happiness deep in my gut. I was on the precipice of love and ready to jump. What would she say? *Pause.*

I froze the memory. Jen's smile. *Save.* Her laugh. *Save.* Both have been backed up, copied, and then backed up again.

Who knew aliens could be so boring?" She snorted. "They traveled all this way just to find a good parking space."

In the rearview, I could see the ship hovering high over the city. A magnificent silver coin that on most days eclipsed the sun. One day they just appeared as if straight out of a fifties pulp. Most people were surprised- except the types who frequented cult drive-in films or maybe the barefoot sprout munching conspiracy theorists. I was neither.

The Ambassadors only wanted the broken ones, people damaged by birth or life. Those whose bodies rejected them, with glass bones or misplaced limbs. The leftovers with named syndromes and disorders that few seldom chose to learn. Those thrust away from society, isolated from the shame of parents, to be hidden in the anemic cheeriness of a state-run facility. Come in, they said, come in, come in, come in.

P rocess.

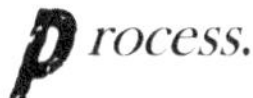

I was beyond repair. A perfect specimen to reconstruct from the inside out. That slick winter highway robbed me of all my feeling. *Access mnemonic data.* There was ice, glistening black, a trick of the light. We swerved. The eighteen-wheeler failed to notice. Contact.

Remembering the world spinning remarkably fast, a blur, like torrential rain on a watercolor painting. The shearing of metal as if the car was merely a can. So much noise that I felt more than I heard. A hollow thunderous roar as if someone drained away its ferocity and left the echo of its sound. It seeped through the fog of my fractured mind. My searching hand needed to feel Jen. Was she all right?

Then nothing. Blessedly nothing. *Delete.* Are you sure? Yes or No? *NO. Save.*

P *rocess. Remember Dad. Play.*

"Hey buddy," he said as if I was seven again. *Pause.*

Dad was the only one who visited regularly. My friends had long since vanished and excuses took their place. Soon not even that. No one wanted to see me in this imitation existence of catheters and caregivers. I became an anecdote. A warning. It would have been easier to die than be forgotten. Even Jen rarely came anymore.

He fluffed the tired pillows supporting my tired head. His face was thinner than it should be. His sunken eyes wearier than mine. Maybe it was this hospital room that stunk of antiseptic and pity, with its sad row of lights that made everyone look this way. *Rewind. Play Again.*

Hey buddy," he said as if I was seven again. He slowly pushed in a rusted metal monstrosity. It was a relic from the wheelchair Stone Age.

"Where did you dig up that fossil?" I asked, putting on my brave voice.

"Your doctors say it's better to get a workout instead of a ride. It keeps your strength up." He grinned sheepishly and advanced slowly, trying to find a place for the clumsy thing. Its wheels creaked from long disuse. "Plus, the power chairs are so unreliable these days."

Electricity had been on the fritz since the Ambassadors woke up from their stasis. As if on cue, the lights dimmed. I wasn't ready to move on this way, to resign myself to this newfound reality. I faced the window, so I couldn't see the pleading in my father's gaze. The clouds churned in a turbulent grey sky mirroring how I felt inside. It wasn't fair that Jen got to walk away. Most of me was relieved. But it still wasn't fair.

We knew this was going to be hard," he said gesturing to the chair. "The doc and I feel it's time."

The silence grew heavy between us. His words, so polite, so caring, hung in the air. I was choking on all the polite. My chest felt as if I was breathing lead. I could not suffer through any more caring.

"Not yet," I said quietly. *Delete.*

Recall Jen. First time. Play.

The first time our legs touched under the boundless blue of an August day. We sat, legs dangling in the pool, swaying from waves created by the splashing of our friends. An apricot blush covered her toenails, mine as nude as the day I was born. I remember how my pulse quickened and I became suddenly shy. I let her push me into the cool waiting water. I dove down and sat for a moment, deep below the surface, smiling as I rested on the cobalt bottom. Looking up I could see her figure rippling through the surface. Then the water funneled and broke as she joined me. *Save.*

Forward. *Recall Jen. Last visit.*

Her averted eyes. *Delete.*

Hollow, watered-down smiles. *Delete.*

False, timid laughter. *Delete.*

Empty conversation that trailed off to an endless nowhere. *Delete.*

"See you tomorrow," She says.

Then bending stiffly, Jen gives me a phony kiss and I taste the lies on her lips. *Delete*

What we had no longer mattered. Our future was as broken as my spine. She was still walking away from the accident. Walking away as quickly as she could. *Delete. Delete. Delete.*

I should beg her to stay, a recollection that still gnaws at my insides. But pride strangled my voice and self-pity imprisoned my tongue. Both refused to let me reply.

*P*rocess. *Recall last day. Play.*

They descended all at once. Riding chain lightning that stretched clear across the Earth, I was told. There was no doubt what stood before us. Bathed in a bristling electric field, sexless and strange. The smell of crackling air filled the room and the startling rise in pressure made my ears pop.

"You can't have him!" My Dad yelled pressing my face into his chest. I was a helpless rag doll in his arms. What was he trying to protect me from?

My Dad's voice was shaking with a fear I refused to understand. The Ambassador offered a kind of peace. To be useful again, to be whole. We would become another version of human. Otherworldly.

"There is nothing left for me here," I said, "What happens when I no longer have you?" My hands weakly pushed him away.

"Don't do this," He begged, eyes filling with angry tears. It was the second time I ever saw my Dad cry. *Save.*

"*W*hy do you do that?" The ship speaks to me from nowhere, from everywhere. "Re-inflict old pains about which you are impotent to do anything? Your species is the only one aboard that ruminates, miring yourself in melancholy."

"It reminds me of who I am."

"Were." Its steely voice was unflinching, unfeeling, yet truthful. "You disapprove of what you have become?"

The computer replays the memory as I open my old eyes upon a new world. Together we relive my transformation. Unmade, I am machine. A biological scaffold for nanoscale engineering. My frame contains more hyperalloy than bone. There are filament tubules replacing my veins and I no longer need air to breathe. I open my new eyes upon an old world and watch it recede from view.

I agree. "Were."

"I don't see how you can appreciate your present if you keep losing yourself in the past. If you are having trouble committing to deleting the memories, I can do it for you. Or..."

The ship places an overwriting cube of mnemonic light inside me which will spin in an infinite loop. Perusing the files, I see my past changed. In my limitless mind, I will be forever in love with a girl who never had to decide to leave. And all I need is to think: PLAY

I delete the cube from my banks. It reappears.

"I learn from my past," I say."What do you learn?"

"That she wasn't the only one running."

The computer plays me a memory that I always overlook.

It's my father on my last day, "These feelings will pass," he said. "You can move on."

"I'm not ready to." I say aloud. My voice speaking from nowhere, from everywhere.

Close up on my Dad's face. "When you are. Or if you can't. The choice as always is yours."

Extreme close up on my Dad's eyes.

I see something I've never noticed before. Forgiveness.

Despite the light years between us, my father is still teaching me and I am still learning. He has already forgiven me for leaving. Something I've never done. I'm not sure if I even can.

I analyze our position though the information is ancillary. My location is somewhere no human has ever seen. As I look down at the new me, I realize, no human still has. Earth from here, is a dim static light lost in a darkening sea of other dim static lights. In the end, I was no better than Jen. We both ran. I got further, but she had a head start. I delete the cube once more and erase the partition in my mind. I feel the ship pause as if to intervene, but the cube remains gone.

Maybe it is better this way, feelings that can be switched on or forgotten at will. What do they even mean to me anymore? These leftover memories are nothing more than electrical impulses firing through a specific group of neurons inside my mostly synthetic brain. But they are also the only part of me that remains unchanged. It's all I have left.

Opening my sensors wide, I turn myself inside out and absorb as much as I can, filling the forgotten hollows inside. I amplify my senses to the depths of space, watching fluctuations in nebula past the limits of ultraviolet and infrared. Outside the ship, the starlight on my skin feels like heaven as I walk through the lattice of the universe. The once unbearable radiation converts into electrolytes that feed me power. Time for me is measured differently now, instantaneously slow.

THE GHOSTS OF *HART'S GAMBIT*

by David Hankins

Human minds were never meant for an AI's cybernetic life. They always broke. Ella's digital silence ate at Jack's soul as he scanned another empty star system in this cursed wormhole maze.

The display flickered and populated. Jack's curse echoed through their forsaken ship. Twelve wormholes? Their odds of finding the way home just dropped from dismal to impossible. A proper nav could have identified the correct wormhole within seconds, but they didn't have one of those. Hadn't for a very long time. The shredded nav station beside the captain's chair still sparked occasionally, despite Jack's best efforts to route power away from it.

He refreshed the feed. Circuits clicked as a cooling fan died, but the display remained unchanged. Power cycled without warning and *Hart's Gambit* shuddered. A light popped over the empty nav station, deepening the cabin's gloom. Jack twitched in sympathy with the ship's pain but didn't otherwise notice.

Twelve choices. Any wormhole could take them home or drop them into the heart of a Ciriac colony. The enemy was fast, cunning, and ruthless in its hunt of the *Gambit*. He'd lost count of how many times they'd narrowly escaped death, or worse—capture.

"Do you see the light?" He prayed that Ella would answer. She alone saw the light—likely a sign of her madness—but without a proper nav system, she was their only guide. Wormholes reset after every transit, shifting destinations at seeming random, so nobody traveled without redundant navs. Jack hadn't realized what he'd overwritten in his rush to upload Ella's consciousness into the AI before she died.

God, he missed her.

"Number seven." Her digitized voice rang calm and clear, as she'd sounded in life, twisting his heart with joy as he adjusted course.

Some minds became delusional and paranoid when they uploaded, while others shut down entirely. It was why such transfers were forbidden, unthinkable—despite their simplicity after neural implants become standard. Ella was often unresponsive inside the AI, but she always returned to him. Her will was strong—stronger than his.

She took over Jack's calculations, correcting several errors without comment. Her math was better too. That's why she'd been their navigator.

A klaxon blared, jolting Jack. Multiple contacts from wormhole seven. Twelve million kilometres, drifting lazily at low velocity.

Fury and fear exploded through Jack. How had the Ciriac found them *again*?

He flashed over the controls, spinning the *Gambit* back the way they'd come. Ella smoothly corrected his reversal, pin-wheeling them back toward wormhole seven and locking him out. *Hart's Gambit* groaned in protest.

Jack slammed impotently against Ella's lockout. "Those are Ciriac ships! You're heading right for them!"

The *Gambit* had encountered no others in this endless wormhole maze, finally answering the Fermi Paradox. Humanity was not alone, and the enemy was hungry.

"They are the light that will lead us home."

"*What?* We've been following your light for years ... and it's the *Ciriac?*"

"They are not your enemy."

No. God, no. Ella's madness was worse than he had thought.

Ella went silent, and Jack worried that she'd crashed again. Only her iron grip on the controls indicated awareness.

Their years together in this labyrinth tempered Jack's anger. A little. They had survived this far together: in sickness and in health, despite madness and death.

"Ella, please, I need control." Her silence deepened.

The Ciriac turned and accelerated hungrily. They'd seen the *Gambit.* Chimes announced a comm attempt, but Jack ignored them. He'd heard their lies before.

"Please, love, you're killing us."

The Ciriac's acceleration doubled. Tripled. Pinpricks became sleek ships on the display. They would intercept in minutes, but Ella stubbornly maintained course.

Screw patience. Jack sent a brute force command, trying to cut her out of flight control. She rerouted his command. Jack cursed and scrambled for a software back door.

"Trust me, love." Ella's calm cracked Jack's panic, pulling him from the brink of impassioned calamity. He teetered on the edge then embraced his fear. Fear kept him alive.

"We won't survive!"

"Let the light guide us."

"Your 'light' will kill us before we transit!"

"We're already dead. I want to go home."

Jack twitched, mind quavering. Ella was dead, but he continued on. He'd promised to take her home. That was why he'd uploaded her into the AI in her final moments.

Ella faded away again like the dying breath of Jack's fractured soul. A system glitch, her mind breaking once more. He hated the glitches, but this one granted him control.

The Ciriac slowed as they neared, silver sharks in a sea of darkness salivating over a tasty morsel. More ships appeared behind the *Gambit*, though the klaxon didn't sound. They must have come from another wormhole. He was trapped.

They couldn't turn back, so they'd go through. Escape the Ciriac, save Ella, and find the way home.

Hart's Gambit jumped when he redlined the engines. Structural protests rattled his bones and alarms echoed through empty corridors. Gravity passed the safety margin, but Jack remained focused. Not even the acrid pop and burn of overworked circuits distracted him.

He would get Ella home. She'd chosen him over a life of luxury and privilege as heiress to the immense Hart fortune. They'd fallen in love and stolen her father's flagship, escaping to the stars. Jack laughed bitterly. *Hart's Gambit*, their chance for happiness.

Memories of her quirked smile made his entire being ache. How had someone so beautiful, so pure of soul, wanted him? He was nobody, a kid from the slums who got lucky in a scholarship contest to study cybernetics. Their love had killed her. He had killed her. He hadn't seen the meteorite shower that shredded their primary nav, punctured the hull, and killed Ella. Then he'd wiped the secondary nav to save her mind, damning them to wander the stars.

He was a fool.

Proximity alarms tore Jack from his melancholy. Enemy tractors clutched at the *Gambit* and the comm chimed insistently. He wrenched the ship aside. Steel and ceramic protested his rough handling, and something crashed down in cargo, but *Hart's Gambit* slipped past the Ciriac.

"Yes!" His elation was lost in the tumult of abused engines. Harmonic vibrations rose ancient dust from the deck, choking the air. A gentler adjustment brought them back on course, and he fed Ella's calculations into the wormhole drive.

"One final sunset over the Rockies, that's all I ask. Take me home, Jack."

Ella's dying words made him fumble his final numbers. Damn those echoes of the past. Had she spoken or was it his memory? He frantically adjusted his math as they hit the wormhole at speed. Fear and hope wrenched at him.

The stars spiraled, and *Hart's Gambit* dropped into the otherness of wormhole space, a bizarre place of twisting time. Rattling bones went silent, dust settled, and peace overwhelmed Jack.

It was time for the dreams.

His eyes opened to his favorite memory: that silly masquerade ball Ella had dragged him to at university. Twinkling lights glowed over dancers cavorting in fancy dress—college kids playing at maturity. Jack grinned, social awkwardness and displacement at odds with his joy at hearing true voices again.

A hint of roast turkey and spiced wine wafted past, and Jack inhaled sharply. Remembered flavors made him salivate and he savored his bittersweet longing for a happier time. He craved these moments, brief respites when memory overwhelmed reality. God bless the weird normality of wormhole space.

"Hey, lover, where'd you go?"

Cheap shoes squeaked as Jack turned toward Ella. She looked radiant. Her spiky black hair cleverly coiffed to accent an ethereal gossamer dress. The entire ensemble hinted at birds in flight. His insides churned happily at her smiling eyes.

He quirked a wry grin, as he'd done that night, and said, "Just trying to keep us alive, gorgeous. Would you believe that exploring the galaxy isn't all wine and roses?"

Ella laughed and hugged him as she always did in this memory, though his words differed from the lame joke he'd originally tried. Athletic arms pulled him close, her body melding into his own, giving life to his dreams. He drank her in. Ella pulled back then wiped away his smile with a kiss that buckled his knees.

That was exactly as he remembered. He might have fallen if they hadn't held each other so tightly. Jack gasped hungrily when they came up for air.

"I love you so much," he said. "I'm sorry you died."

Ella's glory dimmed, and she cocked her head. "I love you too, goofball. We're almost home, so don't turn maudlin now. I believe in you."

That wasn't part of the memory. Jack's throat went dry. Wormhole space bent time and reality. Were these shared memories, or his alone?

"Why put your faith in me? I killed you."

Her warm eyes held no accusation. "It was an accident. I've never regretted our time together. You are my life, my soul, my lov—"

Wormhole space ruptured into reality. Jack screamed at the Universe as Ella was torn from him again.

"Beginning analysis." Her mechanical voice felt cold and dark after the vibrancy of wormhole space's otherness. Jack clutched at his shattered soul and focused on the display. Yellow sunlight pierced the viewport, casting the ragged cabin in sharp relief as system details filtered in.

G2 primary, eight planets, four of them gas giants. The third planet lay closest, slightly to port from their current heading. Deep space and orbital infrastructure populated the display, though no ships. A dead Ciriac colony?

A clipped male voice crackled on the speaker. "Unknown vessel, identify yourself." The tricky Ciriac had overridden his comm lockout. Jack scanned the display. Where were they? The line stayed open, and a woman yelled in the background.

"That's *Hart's Gambit*! The transponder—"

"Is wrong. They were declared lost two centuries ago."

"What about the ghost-ship sightings? There are over ninety-three confirmed—"

The line died. Jack twitched, refreshing his feed to scan for wormholes, for the way home. Still no sign of the Ciriac, despite the comm call.

The woman's voice returned with a note of concern which sounded genuine, catching Jack's attention. "*Hart's Gambit*, do you read me? Please respond. Please."

The voice sparked something in Jack's mind. Curiosity, clarity—he wasn't sure. He tried to respond, but his voice found only silence, the comm transmitter destroyed long ago with the nav.

No matter. The voices were scrambled echoes of the past. He focused on finding wormholes. Therein lay safety and the way home. Therein lay Ella, and the memories he craved.

Faulty sensors cycled, and Ciriac ships snapped onto his display. A hive of bustling activity spiked Jack's nerves. Those cursed sensors had worked longer than they should have before turning glitchy. Their failure had just killed him.

Like they'd killed Ella. God, he missed her.

"Welcome home, Jack." Ella's warm voice pierced his concentration. Her tone purred with life and longing—some deep part of her mind having surfaced.

"This isn't home. It's a trap."

"That's Earth. We made it!"

"Can't be! There are Ciriac ships everywhere."

"Open your eyes, Jack! Those are human ships."

"Oh, love, that's your madness talking. The enemy—"

"Doesn't exist! I've faded, but I didn't go mad. Your mind fractured when you uploaded."

Jack's thoughts skittered, scrambling for an anchor. "I... I'm not..."

"You uploaded 172 years ago and have run from human ships ever since, thinking them enemies. But we're home now. Safe."

"No, the Ciriac—"

"Are not real! They never were."

"Lies!" Jack's mind spiraled.

The next wormhole appeared on the display, hiding behind the third planet. Jack changed course and accelerated, pushing Ella's ridiculous words aside. She tried to take control, but he tightened his grip.

"Jack, let go! You have to stop!"

"No! We need to escape!"

"*Hart's Gambit*, come in." The woman sounded frantic. "I've confirmed your transponder. My God, where have you been all these years?"

Ella slammed herself between Jack and the flight controls, locking him out. She flipped the ship for deceleration and it shuttered violently. An engine strut snapped under the strain, releasing a whipsaw of steel and plasma that consumed the portside engine. Fire raged, and *Hart's Gambit* tumbled planetward.

"*Hart's Gambit*, do you read me? Get control or you'll burn in!"

The Ciriac always used recorded human transmissions, but Jack had learned their tricks. He ignored the woman's voice and fought for control of the tumbling ship. They had to escape. He had to get Ella home.

"*Hart's Gambit*, abort entry. Abort!"

Atmosphere broke around them in fire and thunder. Jack screamed as the heat burned through shielding designed only for the cold emptiness of space. The raging torrent of entry drowned the Ciriac voice. The *Gambit* shot over a broad blue-green ocean and burned across the sky like Heaven's final fury. A verdant continent slid beneath them before they slammed into a massive ridgeline and Jack's world became a scrambled cacophony of stone, snow, and darkness.

Jack regained consciousness slowly, his mind fuzzy. Ella rested dimly beside him in the AI, the remnant of her soul flickering in time with the ship's dying power. He accessed the single working exterior camera.

Mountains greeted him, snow-capped and majestic, rimmed in orange sunset. The day's final rays glittered through wind-swept snow wisping off the ridge. Shadows gathered on the near side, contrasting high clouds which reflected the sun's dying glow. The sight sparked a memory. Jack knew those mountains. Was Ella right? Had they found Earth? He struggled against a heaviness that clouded his thoughts.

Circuits failed and aircraft hovered into view. Fear surged through Jack with urgent focus.

"We have to escape. The Ciriac are coming." He sent commands to unresponsive systems.

"Thank you, Jack. I've missed that sunset." Peace radiated from Ella. She dimmed, her electronic soul pulsing as he struggled to focus. Broken pathways sent him skittering from thought to thought. They'd crashed. There was no escape. He'd failed.

"I'm sorry, love. I tried to get you home."

"You did, even though you can't see it." Ella's voice was soft, happy. "I love you, Jack. You saved my soul in the AI, despite the danger. Then your body aged and you joined me before you died, knowing it would break you. It's been a helluva ride, love, but it's time to let go."

Warm comfort spread from her, and Jack felt himself relaxing as he never did outside of wormhole space. Perhaps he could let go, let it all end. Ella's happiness was enough.

"*Hart's Gambit*, do you read me? Rescue crews are en route. We're coming to get you."

The man's voice splintered Jack's peace. Sparks crackled as a power relay failed, plunging the ship and his mind into darkness.

Safety was an illusion. The Ciriac were coming.

An impact shook the ship then a cutting torch flared through the crumpled hatch. Liquid fire carved a hole, and the hatch clanged to the deck. Figures in yellow emergency suits poured through, powerful lights exploring.

Jack wrapped himself around Ella's core. He had to protect her, save her.

Voices sounded throughout the wreck as they inspected the *Gambit*. A grey-suited figure, likely their commander, entered the bridge with a confused tilt to his helmet. The captain's chair had broken loose in the crash, spreading its grisly contents across ancient control and monitoring stations. The commander knelt to examine a desiccated skull, aged beyond recognition, skin dried tight across the bone. Jack's focus ricocheted away. He didn't want to see the bones. His bones.

A voice called from deep within the ship. "Sir! You need to see this. Cargo bay."

The commander rose and Jack watched him move aft. Jack tried to speak, to demand that the Ciriac leave them in peace, but the comms didn't respond.

"The ship's empty, sir, but look here. Someone printed a coffin. Its timestamp is scrambled, but these seals are old. Really old."

The commander examined the battered coffin, running a gloved hand over words carved into its yellowed plastic surface. Most were illegible, scrawled atop each other in a madman's hand, but his fingers paused over the most repeated phrase: *I'm sorry love.*

He turned to a subordinate. "There was one body on the bridge, but he's been dead too long to be our pilot. Connect to the AI, see what you can find."

It was time to go. Ella's presence had faded while Jack waited. Her absence felt more peaceful than lacking as he gathered her mind from the AI's core.

The empty rescue craft's AI woefully lacked security. Jack overwhelmed it in moments, wiped it, and settled Ella and himself into its cybernetic pathways. He briefly familiarized himself before lifting off, abandoning his corpse on the mountainside.

Gusting winds threw them down a sheer cliff before Jack adjusted for atmospheric flight, leveled out, and turned for the nearest spaceport.

His purpose was clear. Escape the Ciriac, save Ella, and find the way home.

Jack landed near an interstellar cruise ship preparing for departure. He slipped himself and Ella into the programming behind the ship AI's consciousness as emergency crews swarmed his stolen ride. A quick wipe of redundant nav systems made ample room for them, and he settled in to wait.

He fretted as rich Ciriac embarked before the ship finally launched. It was a smoother ride than the *Gambit's* descent. Much smoother. Engines purred and cybernetics sang, intricate systems working in harmony, oblivious to the danger lurking within them.

Yes, Jack had chosen well. He'd let the Ciriac AI pilot the ship through the first wormhole before he wiped it and took over. After that, he'd deal with the crew and passengers.

Escape the Ciriac, save Ella, and find the way home. Nothing else mattered. She was his life, his purpose, his need to carry on.

"I'm sorry, love. I'll get you home," he whispered to Ella's sleeping soul as they burned into the darkness and left the planet behind.

God, he missed her.

ALIEN

by Coit Gordon

Escape.

But what does escape really mean?

I escaped.

I escaped?

This ship carried me away, far away.

To another galaxy.

Where everyone speaks a language so similar.

Yet, I'm often lost at what they mean.

There are endless social cues they all know.

But I don't.

I stumble.

Constantly.

They get angry at me a lot.

Nothing is familiar.

Everything I say is wrong.

Everything I do is incorrect and ridiculous.

I have no credits either.

No way to find a transport.

To take me home.

What is even home?

Was what I escaped from... Home?

There are billions of planets and only one me. Surely, there must be one that will suit me—if I ever obtain the credits to get there. The only currency I have to trade is submission. And I am not the submissive type. Not really. Not deep down in my heart. There's a fire down there. A fire that wants more...

...than to live on this planet where fury is only a half-syllable away.

So, I must choose submission. And compliance.

To survive.

I am young. An adolescent still but considered an adult. Of course, I have felt like an adult since I was twelve solar-years old. I would fantasize about my escape. So many planets I would travel to, soaring through colourful nebulae. I would hover as close to the stars as they would allow without my ship burning to vapour. I would close my eyes and sleep, lulled by the hums and blips of my vessel. I would go anywhere I wanted. And discover all the peoples of the planets. People who would be kind and not judge my every word, pounce on my every "misstep."

Constructs would be deconstructed there.

In my paradise planet.

But I am here now. On this world, part of the rotation. Surrounded by beautiful forests, walking on broken glass.

My only hope is escape. Again.

But how?

The nearest city is kilospans away. I meant it when I said I had no transport. Not even a measly hoverbike to port me through the trees, across the river, and towards...

...freedom?

And here comes the screaming again. One more thing I did wrong, and apparently, it was an unspeakably heinous crime. At least in this microcosm. I forgot to clean up after myself.

I had escaped a cacophony of soul-crushing rebukes from across the galaxy only to entrench myself in more of the same.

How am I this lucky?

Is there no planet, no moon, no colonized asteroid where people exist in peace? Where minor things are considered minor and tones of voice are calm, educating, and forgiving?

Out of the billions of planets, surely there must exist such a place!

Where I'm not an alien.

Even if I am one.

Alien but not *alienated*.

I walk into the forest. A little snake scurries to my right. It is free.

I throw my head back and stare at the blanket of midnight blue dressed in sparkling diamonds.

It is out there.

My planet.

With my people.

I feel alone now.

I won't be alone forever.

They will embrace me. We will laugh.

I used to laugh so much.

It will feel good to laugh again.

Somehow, some way, I will make it to the city.

A kind person will offer me transport.

Surely, there are people like that.

And I will be offered work.

Then I will save my credits.

Even if I have to go without comforts.

What are comforts compared with the expanse of the universe?

I have one goal now.

Not to escape.

But to *find.*

I will *find* you.

My people.

My aliens.

Our world will be teeming with laughter.

Joy.

Kindness.

Acceptance.

And peace.

THE OLD, OLD PLACE

by Eddie Generous

"You murdered me a hundred years ago and I've been dead since," Emily said, slurring the words until the final syllable was lost in a hiss.

She rolled over, the bedframe creaking as the mattress shifted its worn coils. The streetlights shined through the window, countless sparkling gems created by the crisp snow and intense cold. Nelson lay on his back with his eyes closed, pretending she'd only said that because she was drunk, because they were drunk. The old cat jumped and then climbed when it didn't get high enough at the end of the bed. Nelson rolled to his side and tucked his legs up to give Sebastian some space. The cat went to the crook of Nelson's knees and settled in, as if nesting.

They'd met when Emily was in college and Nelson was living in a college town. He'd failed out years earlier and stuck around to drink away a small inheritance left to him by his mother. Emily had been two months from her first placement when she was asked to get herself cleaned up, try again another year. Emily's family had her move back to Tiverton, the town where she'd grown up, but they couldn't separate her from Nelson or the apartment he rented for them in a dilapidated building with only 20% possible tenancy due to structural damage. Everything smelled like old fire and melted plastic.

Seventeen months. Seventeen months of public intoxication and nights in the drunk tank after nights at the Tilton Hilton where the jukebox favored the eighties, and the crowds grew younger and younger all the time. Seventeen months until Emily was kidnapped by her parents and a few old friends. There'd already been an intervention, and Emily begging to see Nelson, and locks on treatment center doors, and ninety days drying up followed by a year out of province where Emily finished her education to become a nurse.

The sun shined painfully through the windows of the bedroom they shared. Nelson squinted. Sebastian remained where he'd been, his body of loose, loose fur like a heating pad. Gently, Nelson rolled over to see the clock on the nightstand. Emily's shoulder was in the way, so he pushed himself higher. A great inhalation jerked up Nelson's nose. He dropped to an elbow after he saw the numbers and reached out for Emily.

"Wake up. You're late for work," he said, his mouth sticky and slimy with the film of dehydration, cola, and rum.

Emily opened her eyes. A moment passed, then another, and another. She sighed and kicked from bed. She plucked her cellphone from the nightstand. Dead. She plugged it in and found that she had three new messages.

"Hello, Emily. This is Elinor Kaufman. I'd hoped to do this in person, but you're again late or not showing. I've spoken with your union representative, and she insures me this is the most I can do—I'd like to fire you outright. Starting today, you're on paid medical leave and you have sixty days to join a treatment program.

"If you choose not to join a program, you will be terminated. As of today, you're off the roster schedule. If you have any questions, contact your union representative. And, after your treatment, I strongly encourage you to seek employment at another hospital for the sake of our morale. Nobody wants to see someone who was once a friend jump off a cliff."

Click.

"If you'd like to listen—"

Emily ended the call and flopped back onto the bed. "You find a job yet, you fucking loser?"

Nelson rolled over and the cat nestled in anew. He couldn't tell her he was terrified of handing out resumes. Terrified of the life a job might lead to. He'd never worked before.

They'd reunited eight months ago. He was out front of the grocery store. Despite the raggedy stubble and his scent, Emily stopped. She hadn't seen him since her family rescued her from that life she'd been living, but who was going to rescue him? How long had he lived on the street?

"There's a shelter so long as you get in before eight," he'd said, as if defending his plight.

She hadn't taken him home to the townhouse she'd bought after her divorce, not right away. She saw him, and it picked at her. Day after day, sometimes at work, sometimes at the store, sometimes creeping the sidewalks, focus pointed to the world at his feet where dropped change might hide. She gave him a twenty through her car window and he nodded, eyes teary—perhaps at what the gift would buy, perhaps over how far he'd fallen and what she had to see.

Almost seven years after their abrupt separation, she took him home and introduced him to Sebastian. They talked and she gave Nelson a key. He slept in the spare room. He never smelled like booze. He was quiet when he snuck back into her home, even fall-down drunk.

At three that afternoon, Nelson awoke to find the bed at his knees and the bed to his left vacated. He kicked free of the blankets and rose. After pissing and brushing his teeth, he went downstairs to find Emily. She'd showered and was sipping coffee. There was a brandy bottle on the counter next to her mug.

"I'm going to help you," Nelson said.

Emily looked away from her phone. The sneer on her face and the disgust in her eyes struck like an arrow into everything vital about his being.

"You ain't helping nothing. I got to look for a new job and you ain't helping nothing," she said.

"I'm going to get sober and help you get sober," Nelson said. Being as sober as he got, this declaration shook him. He put his hands in the pockets of the track pants he'd worn to bed and bunched the lining in his fists.

Emily's face scrunched further, reddening. "Fuck you! I'm not some stinking drunk. I don't need your pity or your help. Elinor Kaufman is a cunt and I'm going to sue her for wrongful ... whatever."

Nelson bent, hunched himself as if he might retain additional strength from being small. He sucked back the tears threatening to undo his seams and said, "I'm going to help you. I did this to you and you're right, I am a loser, but I'm going to fix this."

He didn't look up in time to see the mug coming at him.

When Nelson opened his eyes, Emily was leaning over him, sewing his forehead. He reached a hand up and she swatted it away.

"Almost done," she said.

He let his hand fall to his side where he lay on the linoleum of the main floor of the townhouse. She breathed on him. He smelled the brandy; she drank it with her coffee during the day whenever she wasn't at work. At work it was vodka, little airplane bottles that she stashed in her purse, her pockets, her car, her underwear when she was wearing scrubs — anywhere else, they clanked together and gave her away.

"You're always taking care of me," he said and this time the tears did fall, streaking into his hair from the corners of his eyes.

"I can't help it," she said and snipped away the plastic bracelet thread she'd used to sew him up. "You better stay home tonight."

"Maybe you should, too."

Emily pushed to her feet without another word.

He was woozy and couldn't follow her if he wanted to.

Night had settled and Nelson awoke from a nap on the couch to find the home silent and dark. To his surprise, Sebastian hadn't nestled behind his knees. He sat up and felt the coolness of the cushion before reaching to the top of the couch. The cat wasn't there either.

"Sebastian? Here, kitty-kitty," he said.

He hit the light switch, repeating his call over and over. He checked where the food and litter box hid. He checked the windowsills. He went upstairs and checked the office. He went to the bedroom and checked the bed. He got down on his knees and elbows to check beneath.

"Hey, why didn't you come?" he said and reached in to pet the cat. He stroked the fur slowly, waiting for the eventually purring. "You know, you might be my only friend in the whole world. Pretty sure Emily hates me." He continued stroking, but the cat remained still beneath his soft touch. "Hey. Hey. Sebastian?"

Nelson pulled the stiff and lifeless cat from beneath the bed.

Tears dry, Nelson dressed for the weather. According to the screensaver on the computer in the office, it was -28°C. He stepped into the night. Immediately his nose hairs adhered to one another. His eyes ached. His hands and feet developed pins and needles. The Tilton Hilton was four blocks from the townhouse. Within his coat pocket, he flicked a lighter that had come from who knows where. The streets were mostly vacant. The sidewalks and tree branches shined like diamonds beneath the big blue moon.

Rock music was audible from the parking lot. Two young men stood smoking outside the entry. One said something to the other and both sniggered as Nelson passed them. He knew them to see them, they were people Emily had gone to high school with. Inside, the heat staggered Nelson and he paused to gather himself before passing through the long hallway that led to the bar proper. He had no doubts Emily would be here.

Two women passed him. One said *something, something, slut* that Nelson wasn't prepared to catch. He reached the toasty ambiance of the Tilton Hilton. Some young men and women were dancing while most milled around. Some sat at tables with baskets of wings and pitchers of beer. The pool tables were empty, stalled mid-game. Behind a jut in the wall where the cues hung was Emily. She had on a short jean skirt and halter top and was leaned over a high table. A big man in a plaid shirt and open blue jeans pulled just below his butt was fucking her from behind. Three more men stood watching.

Within seconds, the first man stiffened and arched his back, pumping jerkily. One of the trio watching gave a little hoot. Another man opened his pants. Emily didn't move as the big man removed himself, sticky and shrinking.

Was she even awake? Nelson took three steps toward the scene. He stopped when her hand snaked out to position a small glass to her lips.

The next man started fucking Emily and her eyes settled on Nelson. Her hand left the glass, and she raised her middle finger. The big man who'd just finished turned at this and started Nelson's way.

"You a boyfriend or something?" The big man had his arms folded over his broad chest. He loomed above Nelson.

Nelson cowered and said, "Tell her, her cat died."

"Fuck off."

The man pushed Nelson. Flailing and already dizzy from the knock on the head earlier, he fell into a pool table. The big man snorted a laugh and walked away.

People were looking at him when he pushed to his feet. Most seemed to welcome the distraction from the lurid scene at the back of the bar. Despite the eyes on him, Nelson walked to an empty table. Three unfinished drinks in glasses—brown liquid with ice—and a half pitcher of beer awaited him. He polished them off in quick succession, ignoring the disgust and surprise coming from onlookers' mouths. Emily had cleaned him up on the surface, but he was still him.

Into the cold. Into the darkness. Too late to get into the shelter, Nelson put his head down and walked toward the old part of town. The city had put a fence around the apartment building they'd moved into when Emily first brought him here. The chained gate had been pulled far enough that Nelson could crawl through. His pants were stiff with ice and his body ached all over by the time he got the plywood off the entrance and stepped through the door—someone had broken the glass.

Blindly, moving by memory, Nelson shuffled to the staircase. He flicked on his lighter to see the dusty path before him. He pushed onward. The cold seemed to have settled into the marrow of his bones. He opened the heavy steel door of the second floor. His old apartment was open. He wondered if he'd been the last official occupant.

Unofficially, he'd come back now and then over the years just to see, just to remember.

In the middle of the living room was an old twin mattress he'd dragged up here years ago. Next to it was a loveseat he'd dragged in from another vacated apartment not long after he'd scored the mattress. He lit candles and lay down. When his vision settled, he recognized that someone else had been there since his last visit.

Slushy, nearly solid, he swished the liquid at the bottom of a green bottle of lemon gin. The cap was gone. He put it to his lips. A cigarette butt bobbed against his tongue, and he let it slide down his throat with the cold, cold liquid. He gagged after a moment. Someone had pissed into the gin dregs at the bottom of the bottle.

"Dammit," he said and spat.

He tossed the bottle away and balled up on the mattress. He'd never been so cold. He considered putting the couch cushions on him. They wouldn't stay if he did. He then thought about the time he'd gone to a party in a field, and the fire the hicks had built. It had to be twenty feet high. There'd been furniture in that fire, the springs going red hot. He'd never felt anything like it.

He pushed the old candles within their wine bottles to the edge of the couch. The flames touched against the material and quickly Nelson felt the welcome heat. He closed his eyes. His legs stretched a little and Sebastian climbed up onto the mattress and curl behind his knees.

NWABUNWANNE

by Kasimma

Harmattan kissed thirty-six-year-old Nwabunwanne with its dryness, cracking, not just her lips, but her heart. She stamped her feet hard all the way from Otedola Estate gate to Tunde Pinheiro Street where she lived with her mother. Her Bible and handbag struggled for breath under the prowess of her grip.

That Sunday, she was grateful that her neighbours behaved like Americans: always minding their business and not saying more than "hi, good morning." The only person she met on the street, all dressed up for church, wearing a big hat that looked more like a coolie hat than a fascinator, smiled at her, but Nwabunwanne did not even give her a second glance. She banged the gate behind her just to alert her mother of her mood. Yet, she found her mother watching TV, her legs crossed on the center table, a bowl of boiled groundnut on her lap, her lappa matching the red of the suede couch.

Take Gloria Anozie-Young, darken her skin a tad bit, make her nose and eyes rounder. The result would be Ezinwanne Ezenze, Nwabunwanne's mother, who now peered at her daughter from under her glasses. She faced the TV as though Nwabunwanne was as small as a black ant.

"Mummy?"

It was not kind, not a question, but a growl.

Her mother took her time to meticulously pick her groundnut and put in her mouth. "Ọ gini?"

"He left! That's what! He left without me!"

Her mother opened her palm, her eyes mockingly questioning. "Ehen?"

"Ehen? Ehen, ọkwia? I'm supposed to be travelling with him."

"Ehen go and pack your bags and go follow him nau." *Mtchew*, she hissed. "Look at you. See how you are looking like a disabled crayfish because of common man."

"Common man" their standing joke did not sound like a joke today. Hot noisy fumes like those from a pressure pot puffed out of Nwabunwanne's ears. She knew her mother was succeeding in her attempt to provoke her.

"Is that what you are saying? Is that what you are saying after you ruined my marriage?" she asked.

Two deep lines appeared on her mother's forehead. Nwabunwanne ticked a score. Her mother picked up the remote and pointed it to the TV. A blue line appeared, descending alongside the volume of the TV.

"When did he travel?"

"Two whole weeks ago." Nwabunwanne gestured with her fingers. "And Amarachi knew, and she is only just telling me."

"Hmm." Her mother sighed. "Did Amarachi also tell you that he travelled with his new wife?"

Nwabunwanne's Bible and her bag clattered to the floor. It then made sense why her choir members were looking at her, yet pretending they were not. She had sensed that Amarachi was hiding something more even after she quizzed the info from her.

She wondered whence the sudden angry voices came until she realised that her mother had increased the volume of the TV. She dragged in air, turned, and walked to her room leaving her stuff on the floor. She shut her door and bawled.

Her marriage of two years, plus one year of dating, equal to three years of being with Eloka was blown off by just a puff from the mouth. She wondered if she could have handled it differently. She wondered if that day, when Eloka came back by 3 a.m., she had welcomed him warmly instead of demanding to know where he had been, if it would have worked out differently.

And when he ignored her, suppose she did not insist, would she still be with him? And when he pushed her, suppose she ran into her room, locked her door, and cried, would he have come the next morning to apologise? If she did not push him back, would he have beaten the living daylight out of her? And if she decided to endure it and nurse her wounds instead of calling her mother and crying her frustration, would she still have been married? And it was just a day to their visa interview, just a day! Why did she not just endure?

She remembered lying in her room the next afternoon, unable to move her body, her arms three times bigger than normal, crying and waiting for her mother to come. She heard Eloka crying in his room. She felt sorry for him and wished she could go and wipe his tears, but she could not get up to even release her full bladder.

Her mother came, ignored Eloka's greetings, and walked straight to the spare room where she knew her daughter would be. Nwabunwanne remembered feeling safe and relieved on seeing her mother, but she saw the pain in her mother's eyes. Her mother touched her neck as though to check her temperature and left. She came back with a frozen sachet of water which she placed on Nwabunwanne's arms. The only thing she said was, "I went through severe pains to give birth to you. Severe pains."

Eloka stayed in the master bedroom, ignored. Her mother left that night, refusing to sleep in their house. She did not come back the next day or the next or the next.

On the fourth day, a Saturday, Nwabunwanne felt somewhat better. Her arms were no longer as pink or as big. It was that day that her mother, her parents-in-law, her sister-in-law, and her sister-in-law's husband came. She did not know they were coming, but apparently, Eloka knew because he had come back not long ago with two bottles of wine. They sat in the sitting room, the wine on the center table, listening to the grievances of the couple.

Nwabunwanne was wearing a slackened purple gown. She had since tossed it away from her wardrobe because it reminded her of the day she was the scoff of those she called family; of the shame of telling her story of abuse and being chastised. She remembered bending her head and rubbing the cowrie hanging on her neck as a means of controlling the shame that was so vested in creaming her face.

Her in-laws told her that she had no respect. How dare she ask a man of the house why he was coming back by what time? At least he came home, they said. And he was coming from a meeting, why couldn't you be more understanding? As though Nwabunwanne knew that he had gone to a meeting. It was all news to her. All they said to Eloka was, "You shouldn't have beaten your wife." Her mother sat there, her head bowed down, her arms folded across her chest. When they finished, they asked her if she had anything to say. She nodded. She turned to Eloka.

"Eloka, nwam, since you have said all these bad things about Nwabunwanne, does that mean that you don't want to marry her again?"

Everyone looked surprised. It was a meeting to make peace, not to create more war. Nwabunwanne looked at Eloka who was also looking at her, his face smeared with confusion.

"Because all these things you said Nwabunwanne did to you, it means she is a very bad person. And because you are my son, I will not be happy if you are unhappy in your marriage. So, I ask you, is it that you don't want to marry her again?"

"Mama Nwabunwanne..."

She shot a poisonous look at Nwabunwanne's father-in-law and snapped. "My name is Ezinwanne. And I am speaking to your son, not you. Let him speak for himself."

A thick blanket of silence befell the house. Eloka said nothing. Nwabunwanne kept her gaze on him, willing him to say something, even if it was to say he did not want her again. He looked at her. His eyes had turned red and watery, but he bent down, wiped his eyes, and kept his lips sealed.

"It's okay. Since you cannot talk. Nwabunwanne." She turned to her daughter. "Ngwa, go and pack your things. When he retrieves his speech, he is welcomed to come to my house and collect you back."

Everyone stared at her. Their lips, whether opened or closed, seemed to be shivering but no word was uttered.

"Nwabunwanne, ntị ochiri gị? I said get up from there and go and pack your things, ọsịsọ!"

"Mama Nwa... Ezinwanne, it has not gotten to that. We came here for peace," Sister-in-law finally voiced her thoughts.

"Nwabunwanne, I said go and pack your things!"

Nwabunwanne got up. Just a few seconds ago, she felt she deserved what Eloka did to her because everyone thought so. Now, she did not feel that way. One person, just one person, saw the ill in Eloka's actions and that was enough for her. She went to the bedroom and started stuffing her things into a box. She heard her in-laws saying things to pacify her mother, but her mother spoke only once.

"I am not in support of this kind of peace. You have just taken the stick from your son and given him a cutlass. Since you people say that my daughter is not well-trained, let me take her home and train her. You can be coming to supervise o. When you think she is trained enough for your son, take her back."

Her mother said nothing more. All their hemming and hawing and the preceding pleas fell on deaf ears. Nwabunwanne listened for Eloka's voice. Nothing. She packed every pin she had in that house into two big boxes and loads of polythene bags, loading them into the car. She hoped that Eloka would hold her hand and ask her to stop, tell her how much he loved her, because he did; she knew. But Eloka sat there, head lowered.

And when her mother drove off, ignoring the appeals of her in-laws who followed them to the car, Nwabunwanne kept her eyes on the side mirror. She hoped that Eloka would come out of the house and run after their car. He did not. She burst into tears.

Eloka never called her. Nwabunwanne's mother forbade her from calling him. She promised Nwabunwanne that if she dare returned to Eloka without his coming to her house to kneel before both of them and apologise — promise to be a human, not an animal, and beg to have his wife back — if Nwabunwanne dared return to him when he had not met that condition, she would dig Nwabunwanne's grave, bury her picture in a fine white coffin, cook food, call a live band, and invite people for her daughter's funeral. Anything life gave her after that burial, let her take. Nwabunwanne was so overcome with fear that she dared not call Eloka.

Now that the news reached her ears that Eloka had travelled with someone else, a trip that was hers, she buried her head in her pillow and cried.

ANY TIME NOW

by Alice G. Waldert

The lights to Tim Stacey's kitchen blink on as he enters. With a yawn, he stretches his muscular arms above his head and leans his slender body against a cabinet, saying, "Elinda, pour me a coffee."

A coffee mug appears on the counter under a cabinet. Still groggy, he watches as coffee seeps into the cup. The white cup has black letters inscribed on it, *Any Time Now...* Tim grimaces.

"Elinda, energy snack."

A snack bar drops onto the black and grey marble kitchen counter.

"Tim, where are you?" Melody, his wife, calls to him from another room as he unwraps the energy bar. He finds Melody standing fidgety in the center of a living room with two white couches, she twirls around and says, "I decided to wear my red dress today," then presses her hands against the sides of a sleeveless summer dress. "Do you like it?" she asks with a small smile.

"Yeah, it looks great," Tim says, approaching her, warning himself to be careful; she'd explode if you tell her; it makes her look like she's still pregnant. She combs her fingers through her short blonde hair. I hope going to the clinic works. We should have stopped trying five miscarriages ago.

"Are you ready to go?" he asks, peeling the wrapping from the energy bar and taking a bite from it.

"Almost, our appointment at the Hillborn Inter-dimensional Clinic is at nine," she says.

He reaches out to touch her, but she walks away from him, gesturing as if she is inserting an earring in her right ear, but it's her hearing aid. She's deaf in one ear ever since her older brother hit her on the right side of her head with a quad-room bat when they were children. No amount of advanced technology was able to help her.

"This better be worth the two-hour drive," he says as loud as he can, watching her walk away from him without indicating that she heard him.

The hall closet slides open when he steps in front of it. He pulls out his white sneakers and places the half-eaten energy bar on the hall cabinet to slip on his shoes. Melody joins him in the hallway.

"Ready?" she asks. Tim kisses her gently on the lips and looks into her sky-blue eyes. In his heart all he has ever wanted is Melody, children, or no children.

"Yes, let's do this!" he says, inwardly bracing himself, remembering how Melody had cried inconsolably after their last visit. Their marriage had survived her mother's tragic death in a car accident and Tim's sudden job change. Still, neither of those challenges was as bad as the past year.

While waiting in the doctor's office, Melody grips Tim's left hand so hard that she makes red pressure finger marks on his skin. Usually, the pain would have made him wince and withdraw his hand, but he didn't draw away from her. He feels partly responsible for the discomfort she's gone through with hormonal injections and mood swings from emotional highs to the darkest lows.

Her sixth miscarriage, a year ago, was the worst. Fifteen weeks into the pregnancy and already sporting a small bump, Melody, tired of being prodded, refused to see the doctor until she suddenly experienced pain in her abdomen. The doctor discovered it was an ectopic pregnancy. The fetus was growing in Melody's fallopian tube. There was no way to save the baby. One of her ovaries and fallopian tubes had to be removed, reducing the chances of more pregnancies. Melody fell into depression. The HIdC was their last hope.

When Doctor Markoff arrives, he seats himself in front of them and takes a phone call. They watch his every facial expression and gesture as he speaks to someone through a transparent mouthpiece attached to his face from his ear. "Ah-ha, ah-ha, the date"? The doctor glances suddenly at Melody, "What was your due date"?

"November 3rd, I think." She stumbles on her words.

He swipes the clear screen computer calendar and speaks into the mouthpiece, "November 3rd, that's two weeks from now." He stands up, steps around his desk, and opens his door, "I'll be right back," he says to them and disappears.

Melody turns to Tim, "Please don't let them tell us we have to come back. We've been here three times!"

"It's okay," Tim says, still holding her hand. "If we have to come back in two weeks, we come back in two weeks."

"I don't want to wait that long!" Melody stands up and twirls her hair with her fingers while staring out the window that overlooks a field of green grass.

Tim sighs and crosses his arms over his chest. He shakes his head; the sanitized smell of the clinic is overpowering. He reminisces how his friend Jake told him about the HIdC, 'if you want to feel what it's like to hold that infant in your arms, go to the HIdC. The experience will at least satisfy your curiosity of what it might have been like to hold the baby had it been born.' After Melody's seventh miscarriage, the dilation and curettage were conducted right on the HIdC premises. It enabled the clinic to gather their baby boy's unique DNA structure. Tim scans the doctor's medical credentials, class of 2132.

The door springs open, and Doctor Markoff enters, "Good news! We are now within the required timeframe." Melody passes her eyes from the doctor to Tim. Tears run down her face. She embraces Tim and turns to Dr. Markoff.

Shaking and breathless, she asks, "I ... we ... when ... how soon can I hold the baby"?

"In a few minutes, but first, I need you to sign the contract." Dr. Markoff pushes two electronic tablets toward Melody and Tim. Tim wants to read everything before he signs. Melody picks up the stylus attached to the tablet and signs her signature in the underlined space. "Come on, Tim, you don't need to read every word." She laughs and glances at the doctor, holding a straight face.

"What's this about maximum annual visits?" Tim asks the doctor.

"Oh, that all depends on how the two of you feel on this first visit. We can't have people coming to us more than once a year, and at any rate, it is a steep price to pay."

Tim eyes the tablet suspiciously while Melody presses his left hand, "Sign now," she insists. Tim scribbles his name fast and hands the tablet back to the doctor.

"Well, let's go see your baby!" he says, holding the door open as Melody and Tim walk out. They follow him down a long, narrow, well-lit hallway and stop in front of a door labeled *Spa Room.*

"We'll need the two of you to go through the Spa Room's decontamination center," Dr. Markoff says, then turns to Tim, "You signed up for four hours with the baby. You know you can be there as long as you want. You may not want to give up this chance of a lifetime."

Tim's face goes from smiling to bewildered. *What does he mean by stay as long as I want?*

Dr. Markoff quickly adds, "However, if at any time you want to stop your visit, you press the button on the necklace that the assistants will give you." Tim's face relaxes. The doctor continues, "Abide by the rule, don't take anything from there to bring here, and there shouldn't be any problems. There will be a clock there to see how many minutes have passed. Are you ready"?

Melody and Tim nod smiling like excited children.

"Thank you so much, Dr. Markoff," Melody cries. The Spa Room door slides open. It is like a thermal spa with steaming hot tub baths and showers—a female assistant dressed in white assists Melody out of her clothes. Not far away, a man's assistant helps Tim to disrobe. Melody and Tim's eyes connect with a glance at each other. They donned long white bath robes as they prepared to shower and bathe separately. Afterward, they pull on white clothes. When they are freshly dressed, they stand together in front of another door.

A female assistant stands next to the door, hovers her hand over a button to open it, and asks, "Are you both ready"?

Melody and Tim clasp hands and nod. Their joy is written on their tired faces. "So here you go, Melody and Tim, enjoy your baby. Remember, as you go through the portal, keep your eyes shut. Otherwise, it can be disorienting"!

The door slides open. They step into the portal, and the door closes behind them. The portal's hum grows louder. Melody closes her eyes, but Tim pretends to shut his eyes.

What can be so disorienting about standing in a portal?

For an instant, the portal's lights go out. As the lights go on, Tim sees an image of himself walking toward him. He catches himself staggering as dizziness overwhelms him, forcing him to shut his eyes.

Another door slides open. Tim and Melody open their eyes and step out of the portal. They find themselves in a room identical to the baby's room in their house. The pictures and the lamp on the end table are the same as those in Tim's family for four generations. The carved wood crib with the hanging mobile above it is also the same.

"Wow," says Tim, shocked by the similarity to what they have at home. Melody takes a seat on the rocker that looks exactly like the one that belonged to her mother. She looks up at Tim. "Now, what"? she asks.

"I suppose we have to wait for the nurse to bring the baby," says Tim. A minute passes before they hear someone walking down the hallway to the room where they're waiting. A smiling nurse, dressed in white like the spa assistants, enters, holding their baby wrapped in a blue receiving blanket. She walks over to Melody and Tim and uncovers the newborn infant's face.

Melody gasps. "Oh, he's beautiful," she cries. The nurse places the baby gently into Melody's outstretched arms. The nurse waits to see whether they still need her. Melody is emphatic, "Thank you, you don't need to stay. I have this." She smiles down at the infant. The baby is awake and gurgles. Its eyes try to focus on Melody. "He has your eyes and nose," Melody coos.

"He has your lips and cheekbones," Tim crows. When the baby cries, Melody holds the baby close to her chest and rocks him. She listens to him whimper in her left ear and smells the baby's scent—he burps. A small amount of baby vomit, the color of milk, soaks into her shoulder.

"Tim, hold the baby. I need to wipe my shoulder." Tim takes the baby.

I've always wanted to have a son, then stops himself, *but this isn't real.*

"He's perfect, isn't he"? Melody cries as she takes the baby back from Tim and rocks him on the rocking chair. The baby falls asleep. Melody carries him to the crib, and with one hand behind his head, the other beneath his body, she places the infant in the crib. They stand over him for a long time, admiring the sweet sound he makes, breathing lightly.

"Everything feels so real here," Tim notes.

"That's because we're in another dimension," Melody whispers, still staring down at the baby.

Tim nods and then does a double-take and trains his eyes on Melody, "What do you mean, another dimension"? he asks.

"Tim, *HIdC* stands for Hillborn *Inter-dimensional* Clinic. You know that. This is our house. When we went through the portal, we entered another dimension. In another dimension, this is our reality where we didn't lose the last baby."

Tim steps out of the baby's room into the hallway and peers into the master bedroom. Everything is as it usually is at home. The bed is made and has the same blanket that they bought on a trip they made to Rio de Janeiro. He goes down the stairs holding the railing as he descends. In the entry hallway, he spots the half-eaten energy bar still in its wrapper perched on the cabinet where he left it.

What the hell, he asks himself. *This isn't right! How did they know what the house looked like before we left?*

He picks up the energy bar and eats what's left. He leaves the wrapper on the cabinet and races back up the stairs to the baby's room. Melody is still cooing over the baby, "Melody, this house. Everything is as we left it. What's going on? I'm going to find out." He grabs at the button that is dangling around his neck. Melody rushes to him and puts her hand over his.

"Don't touch it, Tim," I can tell you more, but I don't want you to be upset." Tim lets go of the button. He's trying to read her face. *What is she saying?*

Melody takes Tim's hand and leads him to sit down on the rocking chair. She is staring into his eyes the whole time. He notices that she is the happiest in three years, but something about her is also different.

"There's no need to be upset. This is our home," she nods her head.

Has she gone mad? He's still looking in her eyes and searches for the words, "What do you mean? We were at the doctor's office. We went through the portal." The baby's cry stops him, and he points at him, "That baby's not real."

"It is, though," Melody returns to the crib to lift the baby, "He's the baby we lost from the other dimension. The one we left. We're all together now!"

"Left? Listen to me. In our reality, he died," Tim insists.

"Tim, can't you see he is real in this dimension? Relax, you'll accept it soon." Melody says, walking with the baby in her arms. "In another hour, my breast milk will come in, and you'll see I'll be able to nurse him as every mother does. I've been taking pills to bring on the milk for the past week. It has made me gain some of the pregnancy weight back, but that's okay."

Tim shakes his head and then realizes that is why he noticed she still had her pregnancy weight.

"Oh, Tim, be happy for us. Don't you see? This is the chance that we've been waiting for."

Tim stands up and paces the room. He places his hands on either side of his head and says, "But this wasn't supposed to happen. We were supposed to just come here for the chance for you to see what it would feel like to be with the baby, not for us to experience anything more than that. How much longer do you wanna stay here?"

"Tim, we signed a contract. We can stay here as long as we want. This button is here only if we want to go back. We have the choice now. We've never had a choice before. I don't want to go back," says Melody.

"Melody, honey, we can't stay!" Tim yells and walks out into the hallway. From where he stands, he can see the energy bar wrapper. "This is crazy. We can't stay here!" He turns back and stares at Melody. Her face is crumbling. Tears are welling in her eyes. Her lips are pursed and pressed together."

"Don't you see? This is our chance," she says.

"Look at the clock, Melody. We've had our four hours. Let's go," says Tim pointing to the small digital clock in their baby's room.

"No, Tim. Stay longer. You'll see. You need to accept this is another chance at our life together. This one is with our baby. I'm not leaving," Melody cries.

"But the doctor," Tim sputters.

"He could see that you wanted to make me happy. You do want to make me happy, don't you? He told me a week ago that as long as you didn't ask for more information, he would not interfere by saying more than what was necessary."

"And I never did." The expression on Tim's face was like that of a light bulb going on.

"But what about Melody and Tim from this dimension?" Tim asks.

"We blend with them, Tim," Melody says, "that's what happens when we go through the portal. The longer we stay, the more we blend with them. They're here with us. We become them."

Tim remembers seeing his face coming toward him in the portal. He thinks about the job he worked hard to get and the lifestyle he loved, free of children.

"I can't blend with someone else's life, even if it's me in another dimension, Melody. So maybe you're okay giving up control, but I'm not."

The baby lets out a cry. Tim watches as Melody sits down with him, pulls her right arm out of her shirt to lift it, and places his face against her breast, where he begins to nurse. "I wouldn't be able to do this if I hadn't taken the pills. Now that we've been here five hours, I am almost fifty percent blended with the Melody who was always here. Stop resisting, Tim. It affects the blending process."

Then you're not my wife anymore. You're another Tim's Melody. A mother engrossed in her newborn, which you've never been. Tim shakes inside and stands back. He grabs hold of the button. "If you go now, Tim, you won't be able to come back for another year," Melody says.

Her eyes rest on Tim, then calmly returns to the nursing baby, and she smiles.

Tim nods his head, "I love you, but I can't stay here. We don't know what we lose when we accept another reality."

"Tim, this is the reality I want. We don't belong anywhere else."

"I can't do this," Tim whispers then presses the button. Within seconds he finds himself going back through the portal door. Dr. Markoff turns to Tim when he arrives on the other side, where the assistants are.

"Ah, so you're back. I take it that your wife decided to stay." Tim looks at him, confused.

"Melody," Tim stutters slowly. "Melody, she doesn't want to come back."

"Well, that was your Contract. You had the choice to leave or stay," says Dr. Markoff.

"But, if she's not back with me here. What happens to me here"? asks Tim.

The doctor grimaces, "Well, the universe corrects itself in this dimension. There is no void in this universe, Tim."

Tim looks at Dr. Markoff as if he's speaking another language. Finally, the doctor escorts Tim to the doors of the institution.

"Go home, Mr. Stacey. Melody will be there waiting for you."

"I don't understand any of this!" Tim shouts, and two guards dressed in white approach them. Dr. Markoff holds up his hand to let them know not to come any closer.

"You will see your wife again, Mr. Stacey. Go home. I assure you," the doctor repeats.

Tim arrives home and sits for a few minutes in his car in his driveway. *I left with Melody, and I've come back without her.* He steps from his vehicle and unlocks his front door bracing himself for the silence that will meet him. Entering, he takes off his jacket and stops in his tracks. The empty energy bar wrapper is sitting on the hall cabinet.

As he stares at the wrapper, he hears Melody's voice, "Oh, I thought I heard you come in." With his heart beating wildly, he swings around to see her walking down the stairs dressed in black slacks and a white shirt. He stands frozen for a moment and then meets her at the foot of the stairs. She wraps her arms around him and gives him a long kiss. She is behaving like the Melody he remembered before all the miscarriages. He stares at her, perplexed.

"How did you hear me come in if you were upstairs?" he asks.

"I always hear you when you arrive?" She smiles and tilts her head to kiss Tim again, but he stands back for a second and stares at her some more.

"How long have you been here?" he asks her.

"I just walked in a little while ago. You're acting strange. Did something happen to you?" She looks concerned and watches as he shakes his head, then hugs him and whispers in his ear, "Something must have scared you. Everything will be okay now."

Tim wants to pull away from her but stops himself and remembers Melody's words in the other dimension, "You have to accept that this is another chance at our life together."

HOME

by P. E.

Home is where happiness grows.

Home is a moment, a feeling and not a place.

Most of us live in structures we call homes, but still are a very lonely lot!

Feels like prison in those shells.

Others living in the streets and their hearts are full of joy and happiness even though rock stone is their pillows... home is where the heart is.

Home is a connection. The energy around you, the people around you, the music you listen to, the food you eat. That is home. You could be miles away in five-star environment, having grilled sea food sleeping in a cozy bed but still be lonely with unsatisfactory feelings... because that's not home.

Home will always be in the heart. You may forget it's me today and you tomorrow, kick me out of the building to punish or teach me a lesson. Because of the life challenges I face today, I will leave and go with my home because home isn't a building but a feeling.

Home isn't a place but a state.

Home isn't insecure but secure.

You may call me homeless because you see me in the streets with a bag of things.

If you see me carrying nothing, would you still call me homeless? You may call or see me homeless because I am in the same "dirty" clothes, but do you view construction workers in the same dirty clothes as homeless too.

You may call me homeless because I beg in the streets, but I come from a place of love. You may call me homeless because you kicked me out, I didn't, I won't fight back, I connect, adapt, accept, no complaints. I live, appreciate, and am always thankful for everything because I have a home in my heart.

Home is self awareness; home is hidden expectations, home is unresolved issues from the past, home is one's personality, emotions, interests, needs, desires, self perceptions, and self esteem. These determine each individual's definition of home

Sometimes I ask myself is home a hierarchy thing. Is it like the big dogs have it all, if I lack broader shoulders and a fat wallet do I not get to have a home? Leave alone the immaculate, beautiful untouchable homes worth billions. Or are we living in a society that will put homes first and care for everyone!?

Not until we appreciate each other's self awareness and address self awareness as a mine factor in our being homely, start to emphatically face home matters and put aside the status quo that home will matter. Until then we will continue to be homeless. Question: Do we really need the big spaces that we strive for!? Or would we be at peace in a manageable minimum space?

At the end of the day both the rich and poor all have one, two or three plates maximum in one sitting trying to fill this strange container that has openings at both ends and never gets filled up. This container determines and affects your thoughts, way of life and at the end of the day it guides in deciding the home of your dreams. End of the day... we all need to get together and live as one big family in one home. Just remember what's good for the goose is good for the gander. Peace.

ACKNOWLEDGEMENTS

I proposed this project when I had a different brain. One that was the lighthouse, not the fog. Then Covid changed the way my mind, my body, my memories, and my passions were built and scaffolded. There were moments when I was sure I would have to step away from this collection. But a creative support system, one fostered by Renaissance Press, filled the spaces I couldn't.

Of special note, Nathan Fréchette—the renaissance man of Renaissance Press—has met me where I am. Once, at a protest, I participated in the people's microphone. We weren't allowed to use any amplification equipment, so instead we repeated back into the crowd. With that wave of sound, every word spoken could be heard by all. Nathan is like that. He amplifies unheard voices into the crowd, so no one's words are missed.

Working with him is a team whose dedicated efforts allowed me to keep on keeping on. Of note are Jen Desmarais, who connected with the contributors and managed production timelines, and copy-editors Molly Desson and Joel Balkovec, who took my enthusiastic virtual conversation and used it to gently hone this collection. The commitment they brought to elevating the storytellers cannot be overstated. The extended team, the village that raised this anthology, includes Manda (the sales force), Gauvin (printer extraordinaire), and ListDistCo (our distributor).

Beyond that, we are part of a larger literary community. I would like to thank: the Al Purdy A-frame Association, who welcomed me as writer-in-residence during a year that needed such a pause; the League of Canadian Poets, a collective who delights in words and those who bend them; the Canada Council for the Arts, who provided resources for this project and for so many others; and the Literary Press Group, who have created a space for small press to grow big ideas.

Speaking of big ideas, to the storytellers I offer gratitude for transporting, teaching, reminding, inspiring, and speaking up. Your stories are a gift and they are appreciated.

On a personal note, I would like to thank everyone who let me couch surf at their place, who spotted me when I was strapped, or who offered me a meal when I was running on empty. To the Calhouns, the Bunns, the Cairns, Alex, Zeus, Break, Roger, Pab & Shane, and Monika & Doug, thanks for a roof and a bed. To Ms. Pong, LOFT, Youthlink, and a half dozen high school guidance counsellors and therapists, thanks for doing the hard work of tying my tapestry back together.

To Joh, thanks for mailing me stamps before cell phones were a thing. To the team at my gentle and joyous day job, thanks for helping me remember that a poet can like a good dad joke. To Rehana and Cassandra, thanks for helping me rebuild my idea of family. To the Cassuttavies, thank you for being the reason I can say, "I'm going home for the holidays."

And to Graeme, always to Graeme, thank you for being the safe place I land, no matter how steep the fall. I love you.

H. E. Casson

GLOSSARY

This is an unusual glossary. In truth, it is a glossary of one word: homeless. As this collection was gathered, it became clear that this one word is the gateway to a broad spectrum of experiences. I realized this when I was creating our call for submissions. How should I define homelessness? Do I use the definitions created by organizations that work with folks experiencing this phenomena? Do I use the colloquial definitions that grew within our communities that were, and are, experiencing it? Do I create my own? The answer to all of these questions was: yes. Homelessness is not one experience, and it never has been. It's always been a diverse, rich, and wildly creative word. It is a word that is about absence. As such, it is a word that can only be understood from the inside, where that absence lives.

Imagine my delight at finding Frederick Niven, Stompin' Tom Connors, and Al Purdy in the Wikipedia sub-category: Notables who have hoboed. Imagine my distress as writer after writer emailed me and asked, "do my experiences *really* count as homelessness?"

Inevitably, they did.

As a result, it felt delinquent to publish this collection and not address *some* of what the spectrum of homelessness looks like. So, for the reader, we provide this incomplete glossary of terms that folks—

both professional and experiential—have used to describe humans who are unhoused. It is my hope that it grows, rather than shrinks, your understanding of homelessness. There are as many experiences of homelessness as there are of one-bedroom-apartment-ness or six-bedroom house-ness. Here are a few of them:

At risk of homelessness—this definition of homelessness was created, in part, as an effort to prevent more folks from joining the other definitions. It helps us address questions like: what events lead to homelessness? What communities of humans are especially vulnerable to it, and why? What are the early intervention opportunities that can prevent these folks from shifting across the spectrum to other, more intractable, experiences of homelessness? What disparities contribute to it? It has a lot to do with research and prevention, but it's also about folks' real-life experiences. This is the place where intervention is fastest and where it's most effective.

Couch surfing—this tactile and kinaesthetic name describes one of the meanings most folks instinctively lean toward: a person without a home is provided temporary shelter by someone who offers them short-term accommodations in a space that is neither permanent, nor reliable. Often it is a reprieve from sleeping rough. There is no guarantee that these spaces are offered safely or that they extend for any period of time. Using these spaces may leave people vulnerable to interpersonal exploitation or abuse.

Emergency sheltered—this category can range from folks escaping disasters or violence, to displaced people, to those accessing seasonal, charitable overnight shelters. Different emergency shelters may present different criteria that determines who can access their services. These services are usually responsive, rather than preventive or holistic.

Hidden/invisible homelessness—much like couch surfing, these words are used to describe people who may be provisionally or precariously housed. These people may have a roof over their heads, but they have no assurance that the roof will continue to be available. They have little or no financial or social sway over the shelter they access. People who are counted among those termed hidden or invisibly homeless may be staying, temporarily, with friends, family, or acquaintances. They may not be included in local or national counts of people experiencing homelessness. Often, their friends, co-workers, and family do not know that they are homeless. Some estimates conclude that there are three or more people experiencing hidden/invisible homelessness for every one person experiencing the more easily monitored types of homelessness.

Homelessness—this word is a broad, encompassing term that acts as a parent to all the others. Some organizations have moved away from using this term to define such a broad group of human experiences, while others have embraced it. Many homeless folks use it to the exclusion of others. Many homeless folks never use it. In this collection, we allowed storytellers to use their own words to define their experiences. We acknowledge that homelessness is a word that invites interpretation, rather than restricts it.

Neighbour/community member—while there are many words that may be used to describe different experiences of being unhoused or homeless, it is important to remember that all homeless people are a part of your community. They have been your neighbours, are your neighbours, and continue to be your neighbours.

Precariously housed/provisionally accommodated—community members who are temporarily sheltered may be referred to as precariously housed or provisionally accommodated. This can indicate that shelter is interim, that it is transitional, or that it is conditional. While this type of housing can provide a reprieve from sleeping rough or living in conditions not intended for human occupation, it is neither secure nor permanent. Often, impermanence is an acknowledged feature of precarious housing. Examples include transitional group homes and refugee camps. While there are nuances that separate them, precariously housed and provisionally accommodated are often used interchangeably.

Sleeping rough—this is the definition of homelessness you may have spent the most time with. It is also known as rough sleeping, unhoused, or unsheltered. Homeless encampment communities are usually included in this definition, as are isolated individuals who crash in parks, in valleys, and in other places not intended for human survival. Communities are often created by folks who sleep rough. Popularly, the are called encampments, but folks within these communities may define them differently.

ABOUT THE EDITOR

H. E. Casson

H. E. Casson is a queer, disabled/mad poet, voice actor, and storyteller. They have lived in every borough of Toronto (Tkaronto), located on land included in Treaty 13 and the Williams Treaty.

They decided they were a poet in the fifth grade, and words have helped them survive and celebrate experiences of homelessness, group home living, and institutionalization. H. E. has supported their notebook collection by working in childcare, hospitality, and the arts. Throughout, they have built a found family of creators, caregivers, connoisseurs, and clowns.

They are a Best of the Net, Pushcart Prize, and Audio Verse Award nominee, with work selected for inclusion in the *Best Indie Speculative Fiction* anthology. H. E. has had pieces shared by the *League of Canadian Poets*, *Apparition Lit*, *The Quilliad*, *Serotonin*, and *Taco Bell Quarterly*—among others. The Al Purdy A-frame Association selected them to serve as one of the 2022-2023 Writers-in-Residence.

CONTRIBUTOR BIOS

Brandon Case

Brandon Case is an erstwhile government cog who fled the doldrums into unsettling worlds of science and magic. He has recent work in Escape Pod, Air and Nothingness Press, and The Dread Machine, among others. You can catch his alpine adventures on Twitter and Instagram @BrandonCase101.

Koji A. Dae

Koji A. Dae is an American author living in Bulgaria. She has work published in Clarkesworld, Apex Magazine, Daily Science Fiction, and others.

Carlin Dixon

Carlin Dixon is a Canadian-Hungarian multidisciplinary artist who splits her time between Toronto, Canada and her found home of Liverpool, United Kingdom. She has been creating since birth and hasn't stopped, never having met an artistic medium she didn't fancy or want to try at least once. Carlin attended Haliburton School of The Arts for a Visual and Creative Arts Diploma but ultimately found it quite stuffy and decided to do her own thing (and she's quite happy she did.) Passionate about justice, the environment, and inclusivity, her work focuses largely on nature, our connection to it, and spirituality. She often works with the earth's gifts and imagery while always accessorizing with a dash of glitter and magic. Carlin sees art as a way of spreading beauty, truth and love while making the world a better place, bringing people together and making them smile, all while simultaneously pondering the cosmos. Learn more about Carlin and her many adventures at www.pinkglittercarlin.com.

Em Dupre

Em Dupre lives in a fluid state of contradiction. For example, she loves getting published, but hates writing bios.

P. E.

Patrick is a Fine Artist from Kenya who explores different mediums in his art. He is the author of Exploration of coloured plastic as an art material in collage, his MFA thesis published in 2021. Patrick goes in between part time writing, painting, sculptures creation, pottery and bead making as part of his poetic journey.

Eddie Generous

Eddie Generous is a Canadian author of numerous books, he owns and operates Unnerving and Unnerving Magazine, and is a big fan of cats.

Cait Gordon

Cait Gordon is an autistic, disabled, and queer Canadian writer of speculative fiction that celebrates diversity. She is the author of *Life the*

'Cosm, The Stealth Lovers, and *Season One: Iris and the Crew Tear Through Space!* Her short stories appear in *Alice Unbound: Beyond Wonderland, We Shall Be Monsters, Mighty: An Anthology of Disabled Superheroes,* and *Stargazers: Microtales from the Cosmos.* Cait also founded *The Spoonie Authors Network* and joined Talia C. Johnson to co-edit the *Nothing Without Us* and *Nothing Without Us Too* anthologies, whose authors and protagonists are disabled, d/Deaf, Blind, neurodivergent, Spoonie, and/or manage mental illness.

David Hankins

David Hankins writes from the thriving cornfields of Iowa where he lives with his wife, daughter, and two dragons disguised as cats. His writing journey began in the oral tradition of convincing his daughter to Go To Sleep with inventive stories. That usually backfired. After years of Just One More Story, David began transcribing his midnight ramblings in an attempt to keep his storylines straight. Children are ruthless in identifying mistakes in fairy tales. David joined the US Army after college and, through some glitch in the bureaucracy, convinced Uncle Sam to fund his wanderlust for twenty years. He has lived in and traveled through much of Europe, central Asia, and the United States. Now that he's retired from the Army, David devotes his time to his passions of writing, traveling with his family, and finding new ways to pay his mortgage.

Karin Hedetniemi

Karin Hedetniemi photographs and writes from Vancouver Island. Her place-based stories, images, and poetry are published / forthcoming in Prairie Fire, Parentheses, Hungry Zine, EVENT, and other journals and anthologies. In 2020, she won the nonfiction contest from the Royal City Literary Arts Society. Her cover art has been nominated for Best of the Net. Find her at AGoldenHour.com or on Twitter @karinhedet.

Kasimma

Kasimma's stories and poems appear on Guernica, LitHub, Writer's Digest, Meet Cute, Native Skin, Solarpunk Magazine, The Forge Literary, The Puritan, Kikwetu, Afreecan Read, and other journals and anthologies. She is the author of *All Shades of Iberibe* and is a 2022 Nikky Finney Fellow. She's been awarded writers' residencies and workshops across Africa, Asia, and Europe. Kasimma has enjoyed, very thankfully, the privilege of learning under the voices of Wole Soyinka, Chimamanda Ngozi Adichie, Lola Shoneyin, and others. You can read more about her and her works at https://kasimma.com/read-online/ Kasimma is from Igboland—obodo ndị dike.

Marco Katz Montiel

Marco Katz Montiel writes in Spanish, English, and music. In addition to a song cycle released on Centaur Records, his publications include *Music and Identity in Twentieth-Century Literature from Our America* (Palgrave, 2014); "El disco 45" in *Cartas de desamor y otras adicciones* (Alcalá, 2019); "EEUU – 2017" in *Copihue Poetry*; "In Praise of José Watanabe" in *Ploughshares*; and "Bobby Discovers Salsa" in *English Studies in Latin America* (2022), a chapter excerpted from his current novel project, *Salsa Sensations.*

Cassandra Mangano

Cassandra Mangano lives in central Maine, where she reads, writes, and works as a part-time baker. Her stories cover a number of genres, moving between traditional fiction, horror, and fantasy to examine the delicate, brittle edges of everyday life and how people interact with each other (or not). Above all, she is drawn to surprising stories that get into the head, wriggle around, and refuse to leave.

David Simmons

David Simmons lives in Baltimore where he has worked as an optician, rapper, electrical estimator and drug dealer. His debut novel, Ghosts of East Baltimore, is out now via Broken River Books. Some of his work has appeared in Strange Horizons, Another Chicago Magazine, Snarl, 3 Moon Magazine, The Manifest Station, Bridge Eight, Across The Margin, the Washington City Paper and more.

Anne K. Spollen

Anne K. Spollen is a part time college instructor living in New York. She has published two young adult novels through Flux and has twice been nominated for Pushcart prizes. Her work has most recently appeared in the Johns Hopkins literary magazine, *Tendon*, the Berlin-based literary journal, *The Wild Word*, and many other small presses, magazines and anthologies.

Alice G. Waldert

Alice G. Waldert is a poet and creative nonfiction/fiction writer. Her work has appeared in Misfit Magazine, Prometheus Dreaming, Masque and Spectacle, Survivor Lit, the Bangalore Review, and the anthology: Tales from the Dream Zone. Her work is forthcoming in Arc Poetry Magazine and Chicken Soup for the Soul: Miracles and the Unexplainable. She holds a B.A. and M.A. from Carleton University and an MFA in poetry from Manhattanville College (2021). She is currently enrolled in an art portfolio certificate program at the Ottawa School of Art.

K.A. Wiggins

K.A. Wiggins (Kaie) is an award-winning Canadian speculative fiction author. Her work has appeared in Lightspeed, Fantasy Magazine, and The Fairytale Magazine. She's the president of the Children's Writers & Illustrators of British Columbia Society, and teaches with the Creative Writing for Children Society. Find the series inspired by "Calloused" and her other works at kawiggins.com

Elysie Willis

I've been writing since I could hold a pen, and horror has always been my preferred genre. As a writer, I've always tried to take the difficulties in my life and turn them into inspiration. My most recent obstacles have made that particularly difficult, but I believe that we writers experience challenging things so that we can offer our unique perspectives to the world. Never in a million years did I think I would one day end up homeless and on my own, but I did, and I hope to heal as much as possible by utilizing what I've been through to tell stories.

Jamieson Wolf

Jamieson has been writing since a young age when he realized he could be writing instead of paying attention in school. Since then, he has created many worlds in which to live his fantasies and live out his dreams. He is a number-one bestselling author—he likes to tell people that a lot—and writes in many different genres. Jamieson is also an accomplished artist working with acrylic paint. He is also something of an amateur photographer and he is also a professional Tarot reader. He currently lives in Ottawa Ontario Canada with his husband Michael and their cat, Anakin who they swear has Jedi powers. Learn more about him at www.jamiesonwolf.com

an amateur photographer and he is also a professional Tarot reader. He currently lives in Ottawa Ontario Canada with his husband Michael and their cat, Anakin who they swear has Jedi powers. Learn more about him at www.jamiesonwolf.com